I
like
you
like
this

I like you like this

A NOVEL

by

HEATHER CUMISKEY

SHE WRITES PRESS

Published 2017
Printed in the United States of America
Print ISBN: 978-1-63152-292-5
E-ISBN: 978-1-63152-293-2
Library of Congress Control Number: 2017943953

For information, address:
She Writes Press
1563 Solano Ave #546
Berkeley, CA 94707

Cover design © Julie Metz, Ltd./metzdesign.com
Book design by Stacey Aaronson

She Writes Press is a division of SparkPoint Studio, LLC.

This is a work of fiction. Names, characters, places, and incidents either are the product of the author's imagination or are used fictitiously. Any resemblance to actual persons, living or dead, is entirely coincidental.

For Liz

For misfits everywhere.

So happy to meet
a fellow YA fan—
Hope you enjoy
Book I!

♡ Heather

CHAPTER 1

October 1989

I F HER FATHER CAUGHT HER WITHOUT HER CONCEALER, THE berating would begin.

"Just look at your face! Dammit, Hannah, it's disgusting, *come on now*," he'd scold in his harshest voice, the one that had caused her to jump ever since she could remember.

Hannah applied the stick concealer to her face like an addict, attacking each puss-filled eruption over and over with quick half-moon dabs and dots, smearing and scrutinizing her work. *Apply, blend, apply, blend. Cut or rip the edges of the dried-out scab if needed. Add moisturizer. Rub in. For raised, uneven spots use a Q-tip. Repeat with stick.*

She worked fast, keeping an eye on the time, worried she'd miss the bus. Her fingertip—the same one that had caused the damage to begin with—helped cloak her shame, filling her nail with a ghoulish mixture of cover-up, skin, and blood that she expertly flicked away. Hannah finished the charade with one last look into her old Princess Barbie hand mirror as the first cracks of sunlight poked through her bedroom window. *What a mess*, she thought. If only she hadn't picked last night, and then again this morning, making this daily magic act even harder.

Hannah gave up. She knew she wasn't fooling anyone. Especially him.

She yanked off her old pom-pom hat, the one she used to tame her uncontrollable hair. It gave her a headache. Big hair was in, but hers carried it to the point of being comical. Hannah took a step back. Yep, it still looked frizzy and cone-shaped, and like nothing her mother would ever want to see. "If only you'd just take care of it right," she could hear her saying.

Hannah was a human pincushion for her parents' constant criticism, and there was always ample room for just one more jab. The pain of their words had settled somewhere in her body over time, gnawing on her insides. If only she could please them. But striving to resemble the shiny-haired, Noxzema-skinned daughters in her snobby town only drove her to pick at her face more, and not even Clearasil and Tame Crème Rinse could save her. And uncontrollable acne and wild, "afro-looking" hair (as her family so affectionately described it) were clearly signs of poor parenting. To her parents, a proper appearance always trumped sensitive feelings.

Hannah shook her head, sizing up her outfit in her bedroom mirror—the one with the hot overhead lights, like a movie star would have in his or her dressing room. She pulled and tugged and sucked it all in, holding her breath, and letting her pride swell for just a moment at the sight of her well-shaped, sixteen-year-old butt. But the good feeling didn't last. Soon the shame returned, crawling up the back of her neck and into her scalp underneath her dark auburn hair, flushing her pale Irish skin crimson.

"Harlot," the voice in the mirror pulsed back at her. "Dirty harlot."

She tried to shut it out, but the voice only got louder. *How could he call me that?* Hannah's anxiety made its usual descent down her arms and into her hands, causing her thumbs to ache. The awful memory from last winter suddenly consumed her: the day she wore the wrong skirt to church.

Hannah had bought the outfit with her babysitting money—a denim skirt that fell a few inches above her knee, paired with flats and a pink golf shirt worn with the collar up. The look was very trendy around school, but just to be sure, Hannah ran the outfit by her mother, who barely looked up from her Sunday paper before nodding her approval. Every week they went through the same drill. Hannah had to dress up for church, usually in a skirt or dress. Jeans were never allowed. It was like church was a fashion show where the parents in her town paraded their kids down the aisle for all to envy. *God doesn't really care what you wear*, Hannah thought, *does He?*

Her mother, for some reason, had stopped coming to church, preferring to stay home in her bathrobe while Kerry, her six-year-old sister, entertained herself. Hannah was never allowed to miss mass.

She hurried out to her father, who was already in the car. She never knew what kind of mood he'd be in, and lately she didn't seem to do anything right. The path to the driveway lay covered in a sheet of ice; Hannah carefully navigated her way across it and around the car to the passenger door, grabbing its handle as she pulled herself in before losing her footing and falling into the seat.

She quickly closed the door with a sidelong glance, hoping

he hadn't noticed her clumsiness. They rode in silence, which was pretty normal for them these days, until they were about a mile from their house.

"What are you wearing?"

His tone made Hannah jump. "W-What?" She clenched her hands underneath her thighs.

"You heard me," he replied coolly, tightening his grip on the steering wheel.

"It's new . . ."

But it was too late. Her father turned to look at her. His narrowing eyes began running up and down her legs, cheapening her. "Goddammit, what the hell do you think you're wearing!"

Hannah could see his bottom teeth cutting into his upper lip, holding back a string of things he clearly wanted to say. Instead, he slammed his hand on the steering wheel, and then, without warning, he swerved to the side of the street. "Get out."

"Please, Daddy . . . Mom already . . ." She could feel her throat tightening as she dug her fingernails into her palms. *Make this stop; just make this stop*, she prayed.

"I said, get out!"

"P-please listen . . ." *Think, think*, the voice inside her yelled. She pulled on the ends of her hair as if they were reins, but the tears still came, betraying her. "B-but Mm-mom approved this outfit for church!" she pleaded, her voice catching.

Her father popped the automatic door locks, the sound startling her like a gunshot. "Now," he said without looking at her.

Hannah did what he said like an obedient dog. She watched the paneled station wagon pull away, getting smaller and smaller. *He's going to turn around*, she told herself. *He's going to turn around.*

She turned back toward home, gauging the long walk ahead. She didn't have a coat and felt like a fool standing there dressed in a short-sleeve shirt and miniskirt on one of the coldest mornings of the year. She prayed that the neighbors weren't gawking from their warm living rooms. Why the hell hadn't she chosen dress pants and a sweater instead of being so stupidly excited to wear her new outfit? *It's February, for god's sake, not May. Geez.* She pulled her arms tight around her body, looking back for his car, feeling more naked and exposed with every slick step she took. Chills crawled up her bare white legs as she tugged on the ends of her skirt and wiped some more snot onto her new pink polo.

They're watching me; I know they're watching me. Hannah glared into the windows of the 1950s ranchers and Cape Cods that lined the blocks leading back to her neighborhood. *"Slut,"* they're saying. She hid her face in her collar, her cheeks swollen and raw and streaked with black bars from her makeup. *God, get me home.*

She'd give it to herself good for this one, alone in her bedroom. Hannah was an expert at self-punishment: she'd beat herself up to the point of torture, until she grew numb and could rejoice in the pain that tranquilized every cell in her body. She couldn't wait to get started. Somehow, she knew she deserved this. It was her fault he was gone—the father who had once taught her how to play cards and climb the tallest tree in their backyard, the same man who used to light up when she'd come bouncing into a room. Now she couldn't do anything right, from her exploding skin to her embarrassing hair. He stormed around the house with heavy, righteous feet and intermittent outbursts over leaky faucets and broken stove handles, setting those in his wake on edge. Hannah steered clear of him as much as possible; their relationship was now non-existent.

He was headed to church. Surely he'd realize his cruelty and show some remorse for how he'd treated her. After all, sixty minutes of standing, sitting, and amen-ing about love and forgiveness has got to soften somebody, even him, she reasoned.

"M-mom?" Hannah called when she walked into the house, relieved to finally be inside.

"Why are you back?"

The edge in her mother's voice did little to thaw her. She found her still seated at the kitchen table, her palms pressing against it. Hannah's kid sister, Kerry, sat perched beside her, slurping her Frosted Flakes and clearly enjoying the scene.

"D-dad kicked me out of the car," Hannah choked. *Please hold me.*

"What did you do?"

"N-nothing . . . I swear . . . he didn't like my skirt." Hannah began to blubber like she was five again. She wasn't allowed to swear, let alone miss church. But above all, she wasn't allowed to cry in front of her parents.

"I don't want to hear it. Go to your room!" Her mother commanded with a stern look before scowling back into her newspaper.

All that had felt good and promising that morning had

suddenly unraveled. Her new, pretty clothes shook in a tight ball on her closet floor. Sixteen years old and she was still hiding from them.

"I need help! God, where are you?" Hannah whispered into the darkness from the floor of her closet. She heard her mom's footsteps overhead and quickly changed. She then buried the denim "devil" behind her hanging clothes, hoping her father would leave her alone the rest of the day.

The front door slammed an hour later, followed by her father's pounding on her bedroom door.

"Hannah!" he yelled.

Her hand shook knowing she didn't have a choice but to open the door. She swung it open reluctantly to see her father's red face awaiting her on the other side.

"Hannah, if you *ever* . . ."

"*What, what did I do?*"

"You look like you *want it,*" he spat.

"What? Wanted *what,* Dad? I don't—"

"Harlot. You look like a *harlot!* A dirty harlot!"

"W-what, Dad? What do you mean?" Incredulous that this wasn't over yet, Hannah did her damndest to stop her tears.

He shook his index finger in her face, looking like Moses himself. "If you ever wear that skirt again, you're out of this house . . . for good!"

Hannah ran past him and out to her mother for help.

"Please, M-mom, you know what happened. You told me the outfit was okay . . ." *Please hold me, Mommy,* she pleaded silently.

"Don't get me involved," her mother said, turning her back to Hannah. She then waved her away like a gnat.

Hannah flew back into her room, feeling like her head was about to explode. She shut the door, sank to the floor, and grabbed her diary from underneath her mattress. Chest heaving, she wrote her screams on paper:

I NEED HELP!!! My father just called me a dirty harlot. I hate all of you! There is no one I can turn to. You treat me like shit! I hate you, almost as much as I hate myself. I'll never forgive you Dad for calling me dirt, Mom for turning your back on me, always. I have no friends because you don't even make me feel worth it. I hate. That's all I feel. How many times do I have to be unloved, rejected, and shitted on? I'm a person too. God, where are you? I just want to die. Please help me.

A dirty harlot. She didn't know what the word meant, so she looked it up in her dictionary, the one she used for school:

Harlot, noun

A woman who engages in sexual intercourse for money. A prostitute.

Hannah gasped. She'd never even kissed a boy. She reread the ugly words over and over to maximize the pain and make herself go numb. *He thinks this of me, my own father? Then I must be one. Why else would he call me that?* Hannah dug her nails into her face. Her fingers traveled upward to pull her hair from her scalp, but the pain wouldn't subside. *I must be, he told me so . . .*

Her head throbbed from crying so hard; her limbs were

weak and lifeless. *If only I was lifeless,* she thought darkly. She reached for her only ally in the house—a cheap, oversized stuffed hippo. She rocked it back and forth, pretending it was her mother—but a different mother, one that held her and made everything better. She hugged the hippo until she collapsed into some sort of sleep. No one came to check on her.

Her father had ignored her existence for the rest of the week. And Hannah had done little to garner his attention, only coming out of her room to eat and use the bathroom. She'd gotten herself up for school and disappeared back inside her four walls as soon as she came home, until, one day, her mother had enough and told her, "Quit your carrying on, for Christ's sake."

Hannah simply nodded and swallowed it back down.

CHAPTER 2

―――――

HARLOT, THE WORD ASSAULTED HER BRAIN AGAIN.

"Not now!" Hannah cursed under her breath, pushing down the painful memory before storming out of her bedroom and into the cool hallway. She glanced down at the wall-to-wall blue-green carpeting with the dust stripe along the edges where the floor met the wall. Some weeks the dirt trail was worse than others. This was one of those weeks.

"I'm going to school!" she called to her mom, but only the burnt orange starburst wall clock in the kitchen ticked back. The house was eerily quiet. Damn it. She could die and no one would care.

Hannah hated her family's dark '70s ranch house and the prison it represented, starting with the kitchen's gold-speckled Formica countertops, its table that held down the peeling linoleum floor, and the harvest-gold appliances festering in grease and food droppings. She hated, too, the brown laminate cabinets that held their hoarders' secrets, along with overdue bill statements, yellowing nail polishes, and half-empty pill bottles stuffed in drawers and away from prying eyes.

Hannah double-timed it to the bus stop; her girlfriends

would be waiting for her. Well, not really. She'd meet them at the corner. Maybe they'd look up from their conversation and say hi. Usually they didn't. But that didn't stop her. *You're trying too hard*, she told herself as she came closer to the corner where the three girls held court. Other bus kids, the peripherals, circled around them, each pretending to focus on something else as they tried to eavesdrop on the trio's conversation. Hannah obsessed over them too. She always psyched herself up on the walk there with a silent pep talk: *they like you, you're one of them, this is your group.* She wanted it so badly. Always had.

Hannah never kept friends for long. She was the kid with "cooties" on the elementary school playground. *It's just a game; they aren't being mean*, she'd tell herself, but it was hard to convince herself that it was true as they sought "cootie shots" whenever she came around. Back then, her teachers would watch, clustered together on the black top, pursing their lips and shaking their heads at the pitiful kid dressed in the hand-me-down boy clothes. The pretty girls in class had worn their long hair in French braids and run around in sherbet-colored dresses, dripping in pink, purple, and peach. Appearances may have been important to Hannah's parents, but frugality was king no matter how much she cried for prettier clothes. "You don't waste money on a kid," they told her.

Hannah's classmates also teased her about whether she was a boy or a girl, yanking her short pixie haircut—one of the many battles she had fought with her mother over the years. "You can have longer hair when you can take care of it," her mother would say.

Hannah had always tried her best to hold it together.

Tears only made it worse. Eventually she'd gotten used to the tormenting and pretended to be in on the joke. The faster they ran from her, the faster she chased them. *Please like me, will you like me today?* she'd pray. They never did—but they eventually lost interest in the weird girl who dressed and looked like a boy, and for the most part left her alone.

She'd told herself that high school would be different. She could afford to wear what she wanted now, for one; she'd made sure of that with all of her babysitting jobs. And she knew how the popular girls dressed, how they wore their hair. She could be just like them. But somehow, it hadn't worked out that way.

Don't ignore me, she thought as she approached the three girls at the bus stop, her heart pounding. *Not today.* In a moment of inspiration, she breathlessly blurted out, "Hey, do you guys know where I can buy some . . . *good stuff*, you know . . . at school?"

That got them. The trio of well-dressed girls, with the pretty shiny hair and clear skin, stopped and swirled around in unison like a Breck Shampoo commercial, even spiky, red-headed Gillian with her half-smile/half-smirk and cold, blue-gray eyes.

Is she laughing at me? Hannah wondered.

But it was the blonde, Leeza, who spoke first. "Oh, you need to talk to Deacon, that cute guy who hangs out near the girls' locker room right before homeroom and after school sometimes. You can't miss him," she said, spouting her know-it-all wisdom of all things high school. Sparkly-eyed Leeza, with her ice-pink lips and frosted tresses, co-captained the high school debate team and was the founder of the school's

Spirit Club—a group of wannabe cheerleaders and desperate-to-be-popular girls looking for ways to amp up their status.

The others nodded toward Hannah, and she immediately liked having their pretty, electric-blue-lined eyes on her. She already knew where she could score some weed at her school. Everyone did. All the girls admired the ultra-cool dealer boy who hung out in the hallways, mysterious and handsome in his black leather trench coat, ripped, faded jeans, and black combat boots. A high school loner by choice, he stood out from all the other male clones; he was deeply serious, with an irresistible, brooding demeanor. He hardly ever smiled, but could create a path of turned heads comprised of both sexes whenever he passed. Even for the popular girls, Deacon Giroux was just too handsome to even try.

"He's sooo cute," said Gillian, looking around at the others for confirmation. They all giggled in agreement—even Taylor, the quietest girl of the coven. Hannah equated her with bathroom wallpaper: lovely on the eyes, but not much going on beyond the decoration.

Today, as every day, Taylor wore a padded preppy headband, perfectly color-coordinated with her outfit. She was classically pretty in that private schoolgirl sort of way; she somehow managed to look polished even with little makeup on. Hannah had always envied her long, silky, dark brown hair and clear, creamy skin.

Taylor's well-bred good looks and fine-boned balletic body set her apart from most girls at school and gave her open access to all the cute jocks in any grade—so much so that she changed boyfriends almost as often as she changed headbands. Hannah had to double-check the embroidered name on her latest boyfriend's varsity jacket just to make conversation with her.

"So, Taylor, how is Jake doing? Oh, I meant *Daniel* . . . that's right, duh . . ." Hannah said, quick to look away first.

Taylor perked up in response, as she always did, heaving a dramatic sigh and fluttering her pretty, coquettish eyes to the sky to convey her unwavering adoration for her newest acquisition. "He's definitely 'the one,'" she said, beaming. Taylor's self-worth ran head-to-head with how hard the guy fell.

Meanwhile, Gillian performed her own eye rolling behind Taylor's back. "Taylor has dated so many jocks, they're going to give *her* a varsity letter," she once said.

For that brief moment, Hannah felt like one of them. They asked her more questions about getting the weed and gave her advice, though she knew that none of them had ever dared to buy or try drugs. She didn't know if she had the guts to go through with it either.

As if Gillian could read her mind, she began sizing up Hannah's seriousness. "So what are you looking for? What kind of stuff? I didn't know you bought," she said, her eyes widening as if she had just discovered the secret to Hannah's weirdness. Gillian loved gossip, and a juicy story like this would keep the vultures abuzz all the way through till dismissal.

Gillian wouldn't appear to be the leader of the group at first glance. But she carried herself with an unwavering confidence that bordered on conceit, which added to her nothing-special looks. She came off as incredibly smart, and was always quick with a comeback. Confrontation was her heroin, especially with her peers; she could ruin a girl's social standing in one verbal takedown. She would expose her victims' secrets and worst fears on a whim, seemingly without a flicker of concern. However when she decided to be nice, you couldn't help but crumble. The boys liked her, and the girls wanted to be around her—or they feared being her next victim. Just being in Gillian's presence was heady and intoxicating for Hannah.

The bus arrived, and Hannah followed behind the group as they made their way to their usual seats, hoping their conversation would continue. Instead, Gillian and Leeza went on about some party they had gone to over the weekend, while Taylor suddenly seemed distracted; she began tugging on her shirtsleeves and staring tearfully out the window. Hannah ignored her. She wanted Gillian and Leeza's attention back. But they were done with her.

Their high school, built sometime in the 1950s, boasted an impressive redbrick Georgian façade with tall columns and a white cupola, inside though it was just plain old, like *Leave It to Beaver* old. Its faded hallways were crammed with kids from extremely wealthy families wearing the latest preppy fashions, as well as alternative Goth/New Wave kids from modest households who got creative and shopped at thrift stores. Hannah didn't fit into either group. But she watched and listened, catching conversations about all the keg parties and "totally awesome" high school events she wasn't a part of. There always seemed to be some big social outing that couldn't be missed.

Hannah shrugged to herself. Staying home and watching *Friday Night Videos* on TV with a bowl of ice cream in her lap suited her just fine; at least, there, she was safe and away from their stares and smirking faces.

Still, she was curious. She knew that plenty of kids at school dabbled in party drugs, like pot—or at least they bragged that they did. Plus, if she didn't follow through on this, she knew Gillian would never let her live it down. *What the hell*, she thought. Her father had already deemed her a slut; her mother criticized her constantly. *What's the harm in trying a joint?* she wondered. Or did you buy it in a bag and roll it yourself? She'd have to ask him. Deacon Giroux. The thought of meeting him sent chills through her veins. If she was ever going to change her sad, sorry life, it was now or never.

———

Hannah hadn't a clue how one performed a drug deal in school—or anywhere, for that matter. As she worked up the courage to approach Deacon in the hallway just outside the main gym, she walked past him then stopped at the water fountain to survey her surroundings. She circled back casually, watching him out of the corner of her eye. She decided to get his attention from behind. That seemed safer, for some reason, than meeting him head-on.

Praying that she wouldn't throw up before she even got started, Hannah mumbled, "Hey," into his back.

Silence.

Christ, of course he didn't hear me, she thought, feeling stupid. *I could barely hear myself.* She stared at the way his dark hair fell over his leather collar.

She began to panic, second-guessing herself and feeling invisible. But there he was right in front of her, talking to another senior boy wearing a letterman jacket. She couldn't stop now. She took a deep breath and poked him in the back.

Deacon flexed his shoulders like he had just gotten hit—then, slowly, he turned toward her with a grim irritated look. Hannah's stomach dropped. It was already going badly.

His features softened slightly when his eyes met hers. He appeared bored as he said in a husky voice, "Hey."

She'd never heard his voice before. Her throat clenched. With his intense, dark eyes and long, feathered eyelashes suddenly focused on her, Hannah immediately forgot herself and became mesmerized by his moody brows. When they were furrowed like this, it made him even more handsome. She swallowed hard as she stared at the smooth skin sweeping across his perfect nose into high cheekbones and down to an angular jawline, reminding her of Rob Lowe from *The Outsiders*, but crossed with Matt Dillon's dangerous, bad-boy look. *Life just isn't fair*, she thought. *No one's this perfect.* Yet, there he was, not a blemish or blackhead in sight.

Hannah mumbled something unintelligible again, but this time she produced a twenty-dollar bill—discreetly folded inside her palm—to show him that she wanted to buy. His eyes lit up, and he casually motioned for her to follow him around the bay of lockers, abruptly leaving the senior football player mid-sentence. The guy forced a laugh, like Deacon had just said something funny, and walked away.

Hannah stumbled after Deacon until they stood facing one another alone in the short hallway, the side of his head resting on the lockers.

"So you want to get high, little girl?"

"Ah, yeah," said Hannah, thinking her voice sounded strange. She broke her gaze from his and tried staring over his shoulder so she could concentrate.

"How high?" he asked, appearing slightly entertained.

"Ahh, I'm not sure," Hannah stammered, still nervous to be talking to him. She felt passing eyeballs crawling up her back. *What am I doing here?*

"How much you wanna spend?"

"Twenty dollars."

"Well for thirty, I can get you some choice, trippy stuff. Would you and your little friends like that? Piss away your Friday night with one awesome hit that will blow your pretty little minds? This stuff's so smooth you can literally sleep it off and feel fine the next day, zero aftereffect," he said with the confidence of a car salesman. "Totally. Clutch."

His mouth hovered inches from hers as he whispered his practiced pitch. Hannah could smell his mint-flavored gum. *Don't look up; don't look up.* She ignored her own advice. Great—now she was fixated on his beautifully formed mouth and dangerous red lips. She barely heard what he said next except for needing another $10 for an absolutely perfect night. *That would show them,* Hannah thought. Her parents and sister were out of town this weekend; inviting the girls over for an amazing time would clinch things for her. It would be the start of her new life—a life filled with school friends and weekend parties.

She nodded to Deacon, reaching into her back pocket for a ten-dollar bill to add to her twenty. Before she knew it, he was hugging her and slipping the special matchbook into her front jean pocket nearest the lockers. Then he carefully took her $30 by enclosing her hand in his. It was warm compared to Hannah's cold, clammy offering. It felt like they were more than friends in that moment, the way his tantalizing smile reached his eyes, his body close to hers. Hannah absently smiled back, still in shock but relieved.

"Hey, thanks," Deacon said nonchalantly, like they had just exchanged class notes. Hannah turned away, walking the opposite direction from her next class, the front of her body still hot from his embrace. She felt sexy. She checked her front jean pocket to make sure the matchbook was still there, the same place where Deacon's fingers had been.

It was too much—Hannah was getting turned on and she knew it. She wanted to relish the moment, but the hallways were filled with students on their way to their first-period classes. Gradually, the front of her body grew cold, like she had turned away from a lit fire. His fire. She dodged around classmates, many of whom seemed to be staring at her for some reason.

Hannah felt like she'd just been kissed. Then all at once, she knew: she, too, was under Deacon's spell.

CHAPTER 3

THE DAY DRAGGED AS HER TEACHERS DRONED ON ABOUT Pythagorean identities, Middle Eastern conflicts, and now *Madame Bovary*.

How boring, Hannah thought, unable to concentrate. She passed the time away scribbling flowers and hearts in the margins of her notebook, wishing her weekend would start already.

Making things worse, her English teacher Mrs. Myers, who made a habit of calling on Hannah, asked her to stay after class. *What now?* Hannah stewed, wondering what her teacher could possibly want. Mrs. Myers was one of the younger teachers at the school, and she dressed like she'd just walked off the set of *Dallas*—colorful pantsuits and Pamela Ewing hair, sprayed high and away from her ears. She applied her makeup with a heavy hand; her mascaraed eyelashes reminded Hannah of a tarantula.

When almost all the other students had gone, Mrs. Myers gestured Hannah to the front of the room and tapped a paper on her desk. "This last essay you submitted showed some real promise," she said as Hannah stood awkwardly before her, shifting her weight from side to side and holding her books against her chest, longing to escape.

"Hannah, are you listening?"

"Uh-huh . . . yes ma'am," Hannah replied, quickly straightening up and clearing her throat. But soon her focus drifted again to the two girls in the back of the classroom who were preventing another girl from getting up from her desk. The seated girl—an exchange student from Peru, Hannah thought—dressed in weird clothes and came off kind of mousy, barely speaking in class. Hannah immediately recognized the standing girls' body language. They wanted something.

"Hannah?" said Mrs. Myers, growing annoyed.

"Yeah . . ." Hannah answered absently, her eyes narrowing as she watched the girl's deer-in-the-headlights expression stretch across her face. Her teacher's eyes followed hers. One of the standing girls suddenly ripped the homework ditto from the girl's desk. Together, she and her friend turned away laughing, bumping their shoulders into one another as they sped out of the classroom.

"'Scuse me . . . just a sec," Hannah said, already walking toward the exchange student, whose eyes were now moist, her lips pressing together behind the books gathered in her arms.

"Here," Hannah said, and she passed her ditto to the girl. "I've got two."

The girl looked up, slightly confused; then a shy smile gave way, and Hannah grinned back.

"Sorry," Hannah said, returning to her teacher's side.

"I *was* asking if you considered writing—" her teacher started.

"Yeah, I write every day . . . in my diary mostly. Why?" she responded quickly, hoping to appease her. "S-sorry, but I'm going to be late, thanks . . . really."

She averted her eyes from her teacher's questioning gaze and was a few steps from the door when Mrs. Myers called out, "Hannah!" She was leaning over her desk, her outstretched hand holding out another homework ditto.

"Th-thanks," Hannah stammered. She ran back and grabbed the ditto before double-timing it to her next class.

———

All through the day Hannah looked for the girls, but she never saw them anywhere. She felt proud of herself for going through with it—approaching gorgeous Deacon Giroux himself and actually buying drugs for the first time. She couldn't wait to tell them on the bus, especially Gillian. And tonight was a perfect night to do it. Her whole family was going to visit her Gamma Mimi for the weekend. Hannah had gotten out of the visit by complaining about the immense amount of studying she had to do. It was sort of a lie, but they'd bought it. After some debate, her parents had agreed to leave her alone for two nights.

Hannah could barely contain her happiness the rest of the day. She knew that tonight was going to be awesome.

CHAPTER 4

GEEZ, WILL TOBY EVER GET A LIFE? DEACON WONDERED, steaming inside. No sooner had he walked away from that last deal, Toby had come running up beside him. *I'm not floating him any more weed,* Deacon swore to himself as Toby talked his ear off. *What a waste of space. Just be gone already.*

His mind drifted toward the girl, the one he'd just sold to for the first time. She looked pretty young; was it her first time? Damn it, he hadn't told her how to take it, to wait and see what happened before consuming the whole stamp. *Shit, she doesn't look like she weighs much—a whole one could be bad, very bad indeed.*

Deacon half listened to Toby jabbering on about some "toasted" guy he'd hung out with over the previous weekend before stopping him again mid-sentence.

"Hey, do you know that girl's name?"

"Ah, which one?" Toby said, glancing down the hallway.

"The girl I was just talking with."

Toby's face brightened. "Ah bro, I think she's a sophomore. Hannah something? Hannah Z . . . Zandana, I think."

CHAPTER 5

HANNAH ZANDANA. YEP, THAT WAS HER. AS IF BAD SKIN wasn't enough, Hannah's first and last name rhymed. Even worse, most people—kids and adults—tended to use both names when they addressed her, like Rosanne Rosannadanna from *Saturday Night Live*. Her relatives told her all the time that her name, and even her hair, reminded them of the character, played by Gilda Radner. When Hannah finally watched an old episode to see what everyone was talking about, it only solidified her mortification, along with her fear that they were all just making fun of her.

Hannah was heading toward the bus after final bell when some boy she didn't know yelled out, "Hannah Zandana!" She had no idea who he was. *The teasing never seems to get old, does it?* She refused to give him the satisfaction of turning around; she ignored his shouts and climbed onto the bus.

Gillian, Leeza, and Taylor all stopped talking when they saw her, and all three of them turned in her direction.

Attempting to act natural, she tried to gauge their mood. "Hey."

"Hey," they replied, their eyes wide and eager.

"So how did it go today, did you *score* some?" Gillian

probed, the teasing evident in her voice as she smiled at Hannah.

Hannah immediately smiled back, caught up in Gillian's glow.

"What was it like to talk to him? Did he *hug* you?" asked Leeza.

"Ah, yeah, it was amazing!" said Hannah, practically bursting.

Their questions kept coming, and she relished being the star.

"So you guys want to join me? My parents are out of town. Got the whole house all weekend."

Silence. Their eyes darted to one another's for a moment.

Then Gillian broke the awkwardness. "Sure, I'll be there," she said.

The others immediately chimed in, agreeing to meet at Hannah's later that night.

Hannah's heart lifted. This was more than she had expected. Walking home from the bus stop, she couldn't contain her excitement. Her life was finally changing.

At home, Hannah immediately began straightening up the house, clearing the coffee cups and dishes that were strewn all over the kitchen table and sink, rushing around like the girls were coming over any minute, though she knew she had hours to go. She threw whatever she could in the dishwasher and wiped down the counters, even refolded the dishtowels hanging across the stove.

Today more than usual, her house seemed to be stuck in

some kind of '70s time warp. In the living room, large, floral-patterned curtains in pumpkin and gold hues cascaded around corduroy couches flanked by hexagon end tables—leftovers from her parents' college days. The linoleum floor was badly scuffed and chipped in the corners. Even the walls screamed neglect, full of random dirt smears and greasy handprints, along with a dollop of hardened jelly on the main light switch.

Hannah knew her home was utterly ugly and beyond dirty. She could light some candles later to hide its numerous embarrassments and make the living room appear cooler, though, she thought—perhaps play some music. Then again, the basement would be better. That way the neighbors wouldn't be able to see what they were doing and somehow alert her parents. Not like anyone on the block ever talked to them, but just in case.

As she meandered around, inspecting her work, she realized how quiet everything was with the house empty. Every rumble from the refrigerator and baseboard heaters seemed magnified. She turned on the TV to fill the eerie stillness and walked back into the kitchen. Her parents hadn't left her a note, but that wasn't surprising. *Good riddance*, Hannah thought. Her Gamma Mimi's house always smelled like urine anyway.

She showered quickly, scrubbing her face with one of her mother's hard facecloths. Her frugal parents often kept the bath towels well past the sandpaper stage. She shaved her legs, then finished with freezing cold water hammering her face to get rid of the red spots she'd just picked into existence across her forehead and chin. Her nervous adrenaline made her feel incredibly alive despite her exploding face.

Finally, the girls were coming to her house. Only Leeza and Gillian had been inside before, and that was ages ago, when they were still in elementary school. That early friendship hadn't lasted long. Gillian and Leeza had been nasty little girls back then, often making Hannah the object of one of their secret games. Like the time they were in Hannah's basement and Gillian made them play the "boyfriend" game, where Hannah had to pretend to be a boy who liked to kiss them and do *things* to them, sometimes under their shirt. Usually Gillian was the mastermind behind what Hannah had to do, and Leeza just went along with it. Hannah would cry when they made her be the boy, but they'd tell her she had to or they wouldn't play with her anymore. Eventually, Hannah would cave and agree to play their game.

One time, while playing the "boyfriend" game, Gillian had Hannah and Leeza sit opposite one another on the plastic-covered couch in the back of Hannah's basement. Hannah took a deep breath and—closing her eyes tightly, praying for it to be over quickly—leaned in and kissed Leeza on the lips.

Gillian watched closely, enraptured. Hysterical screams soon followed, with Leeza and Gillian falling to the ground laughing and rolling around, holding their sides. Then they began taunting Hannah, pushing her down and calling her horrible names like "dyke" and "rug muncher." Hannah had no idea what these words meant, but she knew more cootie shots were coming.

Eventually, Hannah pretended to be sick when the girls came to play. Soon they stopped coming over altogether.

Hannah could barely get herself to eat; her body felt electric, anticipating the night ahead. She decided on a bowl of strawberry Haagen Dazs ice cream as her reward for approaching Deacon at school and for getting the girls to come over. She didn't know which had taken more courage, so she celebrated both victories with spoonfuls of ice cream as she danced in front of her bedroom mirror to Casey Kasem's *Top 40 Countdown*, blaring from her cassette player at top volume.

When she was done with her ice cream, Hannah executed her careful face cover-up operation; then she fixed her hair to the point that it started to look greasy from all of the teasing and hair spray, a failed attempt to make it look like Leeza's. The industrial-strength Aqua Net sailed everywhere, coating her mirror and furniture and choking her into a coughing fit while she blinked back its sting.

She scanned her closet in search of one of the new outfits she'd recently gotten at the mall with her babysitting money. She chose a pair of slouchy brown suede boots that would be perfect against her light stonewashed jeans. She felt hip, cool, and very sexy. Just like one of the popular girls.

Hannah checked the clock for the millionth time; the girls would be arriving any minute. She squealed with happiness, still riding high from the ice cream. She flopped across her bed, leaving the door ajar so she could hear the doorbell, her oversized hippo cast to the side. *I don't need you now*, she thought, smiling. Then, suddenly, she laughed, anticipating the fun they were going to have. Maybe, just maybe, the four of them would become best friends.

CHAPTER 6

7:00 P.M.

8:00 p.m.

9:00 p.m.

No girls.

Hannah checked outside more than once, even looking down the street to see if they were coming down the block. Nothing. Not even a phone call. Hannah wanted to lose it but stopped herself. She wasn't going to let them ruin this night. She'd show them. Every. Single. One.

"Screw them!" she yelled into her bedroom mirror, liking the way her anger looked on her face and immediately thinking of Deacon and all his hotness.

She helped herself to more ice cream, letting each spoonful roll around on her tongue, fantasizing about Deacon and the way he made her feel when he looked at her. Hannah imagined what it would be like to get lost in those delicious lips of his, to be wrapped in his arms for longer than a few seconds. Forget those two-faced girls. She was finally going to do something about her sad, pathetic life. Starting now.

It was the size of a postage stamp, stuck on slick paper inside a cardboard cover featuring that notoriously snarky cartoon squirrel in the yellow cape. It reminded Hannah of a scaled-down version of her kid sister's coloring book, like the ones given on airplanes in attempt to entertain the little rug rats. But because it came from the mysterious, handsome boy in black who dealt "the good stuff," Hannah knew this stuff was going to get her higher than any airplane could ever take her.

She sat on the basement floor and peeled the entire sticker off the blotter, then placed it on her tongue and waited. Her so-called friends had told her on the bus not to swallow (like they really knew what they were talking about), so Hannah didn't—but it was hard for a girl who bit into every lollipop and hard candy almost immediately. She sucked the stamp as patiently as she could until it dissolved. Still, nothing happened. She hung out, watching the clock until nearly forty minutes had passed. Still nothing.

Bored, she lay down on the floor, sprawling her body into an X with her right cheek pressed against the cold cement, her stomach feeling sick from the ice cream. She zeroed in on her old hopscotch board a few feet away, once carefully constructed with masking tape, now ripped and curling up from the floor. *Dirty childhood remnants*, she thought. *Now look at me, doing something bad for once.*

Then all at once, she felt hot and feverishly sweaty. She flipped onto her back and caught a black streak out the corner of her eye as a car's headlights bounced across the basement's window wells. The streak danced off the walls like a Ping-Pong ball when she tilted her head to either side. Slowly, it turned blue along its crisp edges. Hannah smiled and kept the match going, wondering how many colors she'd see as she spun like a sundial.

Dizzy, Hannah began to question how great Deacon's "choice, trippy" drug really was, and to regret the hard-earned babysitting money she'd wasted, until she heard voices. She bolted straight up at the sound of her parents arguing upstairs—impossible, she knew, for they were at Gamma Mimi's, but still she strained to hear a door slam, followed by her little sister asking for a glass of juice.

Suddenly, the sound of someone humming rather merrily commenced. Hannah looked over at the source—and her head jerked back at the sight of a younger version of her mother on the mothball-laden couch in the back corner of the room. Hannah blinked rapidly and tried to coax some saliva back into her mouth. The hairs on the back of her neck pricked little daggers into her skin. Her mouth fell open as everything around her came alive. The imposter sat there like in a dream, her hair wrapped loosely in a bun, wearing the ruffled pinafore Hannah remembered as a little girl. The doppelganger was reading one of her mother's worn paperback romances and balancing a bowl of cereal between her bare legs, humming to herself.

"Mom . . . Mom! What are you doing?" Hannah called out.

Her usually elegant mother answered by shoveling a large spoonful of Fruity Pebbles into her mouth, followed by a backhanded swipe at the milk dribbling down her chin.

"Mom? Mom, is that . . . you? I don't u-understand . . ."

Without warning, someone came at her from the other direction, knocking her shoulders back and banging her head against the floor. She was underneath her father. Sweat beaded on his upper lip as he pinned her wrists together over her head, his right hand roughly covering her mouth. She kicked and fought, unable to breathe, but he was too heavy and hard on her, his legs spreading hers, his self-righteous anger confusing her. Hannah's mind raced back to that icy Sunday before church.

"I buried that skirt, Daddy, I swear I did!" Hannah screamed, her eyes clenched, but no sound came out.

Abruptly, she found herself upstairs in the kitchen, crying uncontrollably to her mother, begging to be held. She'd just fallen off her bike and the deep cuts on her knees bled, trickling down her white Bonnie Doon knee socks. Her mother stood proud and unwavering with her back to Hannah, staring out the kitchen window, her manicured fingers spread across the counter like it was a piano.

A door slammed. Hannah saw herself running downstairs dressed in a white communion dress with bloodied white knee socks, her little legs struggling to keep up with the shag carpeted steps. Her father appeared again in the back corner of the basement on his knees straddling her little sister, tickling her as she pleaded, "Stop Daddy! Stop!"

Then Hannah knew it wasn't Kerry, but her as a little girl.

"Why Daddy, why?" Hannah screamed more, but her lips weren't moving. The back of her head throbbed; her body was still pressed to the cement floor. Hannah opened her eyes and looked up into his—the man who had given her all those presents. Tears flowed down her face and into her ears. Her mother's Shalimar perfume filled her nostrils with its heady fragrance as her mom tenderly knelt beside her.

"Help me!" Hannah cried. But only a shadow came into

view, growing bigger and closing in over her face before her mother poured the last bit of her cereal down Hannah's throat, cementing her compliance. Drowning in the sticky liquid, Hannah's eyes rolled back into her head.

CHAPTER 7

———

IT WAS A MURKY, COLD-TO-THE-BONE KIND OF NIGHT. THE sky swirled in dark greens and navy waves against a waning full moon. The street's canopy of swooning trees plucked at passing cars. A pair of headlights ventured through tentatively, then shut off, its wheels coming to a stop.

Deacon darted around the side of the front door, avoiding the porch light. He rang the bell then knocked. Not a sound or person stirred. He paced and contemplated breaking a window. He ran to the back of the house, peering into the empty kitchen. He spotted a light in the basement coming around the side, and lay on his stomach, searching for signs of life. Finally, he jumped into the well for a better view.

That's when he saw her, lying on the floor. He pressed his forehead against the window and scanned the rest of the basement. The girl was alone. *She freakin' took it alone? Who does that? Damn it.*

He spat, knowing what he needed to do.

CHAPTER 8

THE BASEMENT WINDOW FRAMED THE OMINOUS DARKNESS occurring outside. Sometime during the evening, the sound of the oil burner entered Hannah's jumbled unconsciousness and roused her. Her eyelids fluttered in the grips of an unrelenting vice holding on to either side of her head. She was wet and shivering, and her damp clothes felt like they were freeze-dried to her body. The sour smell of puke hit her, adding to her confusion. *How did I get here?*

She rolled gingerly onto her side, grimacing at the pain that seemed to travel over every part of her. Instinctively, she curled into a ball and squinted at the space around her. Her cottony tongue felt thick and swollen, and there was a soreness in her throat like she'd been screaming for hours, making her afraid to swallow.

Nothing made sense until she spied the open matchbook on the floor. Then it all came back in buckets. Her panic began to stack as dark thoughts launched their assault anew. Soon, an onslaught of stomach pains joined in with the white thumping behind her eyes. She wished that whatever she'd taken would just put her out of her misery, yet at the same time she feared that it actually would.

"'Zero aftereffect,' yeah right. Bite me," she growled. She felt broken—wishing the cold basement floor would swallow her. She wanted to die and not feel any of it. She wanted to be sober and to be herself again—and she wanted it *now*. *Never ever again*, she thought, swearing the obvious, *if I somehow survive this*.

Afraid and alone, she cried herself raw until she had nothing left, and then she slept.

———

A car door slammed outside, bringing Hannah around again. She blinked at the wall clock. It was after 2:00 a.m. *What the hell?* she thought, wanting to sleep it off some more, but her stomach and head wouldn't let her. She needed something— water or an aspirin, maybe several, anything to take it all away. She took a deep breath, steeling herself against her body's unwillingness to move, and attempted to push herself off the floor, but her lightheadedness and the sticky pink vomit on the floor underneath her kept her prone. She began to cry again, holding her sides, but even that hurt.

The sound of branches snapping outside the basement window sobered her. *Don't trust anything*, she told herself, praying more hallucinations weren't on the way. They had been so real and utterly terrifying—her whole warped childhood, but more mangled and menacing. She kept blinking, trying to clear her contact lenses, which were filmed in makeup. More noise. Hannah wondered if she was still imagining things. But her ears weren't lying, she was sure of it; there was someone in the window well. Her stomach plummeted. *What in the world do they want?*

She took a deep breath and raised herself off the ground to get to the wall switch, reasoning that, whoever it was, they wouldn't be able to see her in the dark. Her head spun from the sudden movement, and she held on to one of the basement's vertical poles. The room continued to rock even after her eyes adjusted to the dark. A crack of light from the kitchen showed her the way out.

Her hands felt their way up the stairs and grasped for the wall phone, her body still shaking from the drugs.

"911 operator. What is the nature of your emergency?"

"Ahh, I . . . I think it's an intruder, outside. Someone's outside. I . . . I'm home alone!" Hannah cried, her voice sounding hoarse and tight. She tasted something metallic. She must have bitten her tongue—or worse, she had had a seizure. *Oh my god, oh my god.* The line cut off. *What the hell is going on?*

"Never ever again . . . " she swore repeatedly, hitting redial.

"911 operator. What is the nature of your emergency?"

"Hello! Can you hear me? There's someone outside my house. I . . . I'm by myself. My parents are away. Hello! *Please* . . ." she cried. The numbing dial tone filled the empty kitchen, climbing its walls like strangling vines.

Someone was tapping at the door now. Her mind raced. Where was it coming from? Her ears pulsed. Her feet grew heavy and frozen to the floor; a weight pushed down on her chest without mercy. She turned and saw someone outside the sliding glass door, but the glare from the kitchen's fluorescent lighting shielded the person's face. The shadowy figure jiggled the glass sliding door and tapped again, more insistently now.

Again, Hannah flicked off the lights, hoping to turn invisible so whoever was outside couldn't get to her. She started to run toward a closet with the phone still in her hand. Then she heard her name.

"Zandana!"

Her brain searched for any sort of recognition of the voice. It was definitely male, which scared her more. Unclear what to do next, Hannah couldn't move for what felt like an eternity—finally she crouched down and started crawling to her room, cradling the phone between her neck and shoulder.

Her room was just off the kitchen, and for once she felt grateful for that. She would call 911 again and wait for the police. *It's going to be okay, going to be okay*, she repeated to herself.

"Zan-dan-aaa!"

Then she heard a crash outside. Whoever it was had just tripped over something on the patio and was cursing loudly. Hannah listened for the voice again, still trying to place it. Maybe she did know him—was it a neighbor, perhaps? But in middle of the night, who would be calling her name?

"Dammit, open the door," the voice ordered. "I think I'm bleeding!"

Fear rose up in Hannah's throat. She quickly got to her feet and hauled herself down the hallway into the bathroom. The blue porcelain sink was the last thing she saw before she hit the floor.

Hannah's bedside clock blasted like an annoying car alarm. She immediately slammed it down and fell back onto her pillow, her head throbbing. Her nose ached as well.

Her wonderful mother must have set her alarm so she didn't miss church . . . which meant . . . *Oh my god, it's Sunday morning. What the hell happened?*

Hannah cracked opened her eyes and assessed the situation. Still dressed in her clothes from Friday night, including the boots, she was on top of her bed. A glass of water rested on her bedside table. She definitely didn't recall getting herself water, but she was grateful for it now. She reached for the glass, wanting to rinse out the foul taste in her mouth, but she sat up too quickly for her head to follow, and pain exploded between her ears. She swayed where she sat, the room clouding along the edges.

Then she heard a noise coming from the living room. *Someone is in the house.*

There was no time. Her heart thumped so fast in her chest it made her ears ring. She knew that she had to get out of the house, run to a neighbor's or something. *Where's the stupid phone? Didn't I bring it to my room?* She willed herself to her feet, still holding onto her bed. Her ribs and left hip ached like she'd been slammed into the side of a car. Blood was swirled across her bedroom floor, ending in a wet spot near one corner that seemed to be more puke. *God, my pillow looks like a massacre*, she thought briefly—but then she refocused on her escape and whether or not she could muster the strength to climb through the window.

"There's nothing to eat here by the way," a voice called out.

Hannah stopped. *It can't be.* After a moment her shoulders relaxed, and she slowly made her way to her bedroom door. As she opened it, she caught the sound of magazine pages being flipped. *He's in the living room.* Not trusting her balance, she leaned on the walls as she made her way down the short hallway. She hesitated in front of the kitchen, which stood empty but utterly trashed. Broken pieces of glass were scattered everywhere; the shattered sliding door hung off its track, and a cold breeze riffled through the room.

She felt woozy as she turned the corner. Upon entering the living room she stopped again, blinking several times at the incredible sight of her drug dealer sitting in her dad's favorite recliner and reading, of all things, *Time* magazine.

Without looking up from his article, Deacon addressed her like they were old friends, "How ya feeling, there?" He peered over his magazine then shook his head with a smirk. "Yep, you look *bad.*"

"Thanks," Hannah said, her voice sounding like gravel. She quickly cleared it. "Thanks a lot. Why are you in *my* house?"

"Well that's quite an interesting story," he said playfully.

"I'm listening."

"Have a seat," he said, motioning to the mustard-colored loveseat under the windows across from him. Cautiously, Hannah moved over to the seat, employing slow and deliberate movements. She felt like she was walking in a dream—a really bad one. When she sat, she practically fell into its corduroy cushions, but quickly straightened up to face Deacon. Self-conscious, she crossed her arms, holding her shoulders like a shield.

"I came by to check on you," Deacon said. "When I saw you lying in the basement, you looked like you were in trouble. But instead of opening the door, you shut the lights off and I didn't know where you went. Same deal in the kitchen. What's that 'bout, couldn't you tell it was me?"

"No," she said, irritated. They looked at one another for a few seconds. "I don't really *know* you. Why would I think it was *you* outside? Why did you even come check on me?"

"Just thought . . ." He looked away from her then, his expression darkening.

Hannah stared at the carpet, confused about what to do next. Finally, she said, "Y-you have to go." Her voice cracked, her eyes still avoiding his. "I-I have to . . ." She swallowed back the tears that threatened to come as she leaned forward, jamming her nails into her upper arms. Suddenly, her anxiety over the state of the house superseded how broken and ill she felt, and her brain splintered into hysterics. "My parents . . . they're gonna be home soon, oh my god, what time is it? I have to get cleaned up . . . there's all this blood . . . in my room . . . pink throw-up . . . THE KITCHEN! They're going to kill me. What am I going to tell them? I need to make up something about the glass door—but what, WHAT? They'll never believe me. The house, they just care about the house . . . I'm dead, definitely dead . . . You have to go . . . NOW."

Hannah pushed herself up off the couch, turning from him so he couldn't see her crumbling.

"Hey," he said softly. "It's going to be okay. That's why I stayed. To make sure you came out of it. I'll help you clean up. When are your parents back in town?"

That stopped her. "How do you know my parents are away?"

"Well, they're not here now, and they weren't yesterday."

"Have you been here *all* weekend?"

He smiled. "I saw Gillian yesterday when I was driving down your block . . . I'd gone home for a bit and was coming back to check on you. She said you and your family were out of town this weekend. I knew *you* weren't, so I figured just your parents were."

That two-faced bitch, she thought. Gillian didn't give a flying flip what happened to her, telling Deacon she wasn't home when she knew she was. First she and the other girls stand her up Friday night, then she tries to keep Deacon away from her? Hannah steamed inside. Her anger revived her a bit. Maybe she *was* feeling better.

"Here, let me help you," Deacon said softly, tentatively putting his arm around her shoulders and helping her walk down the hall to the bathroom. "Take a shower, you'll feel better . . . but first, show me where your mom keeps the broom."

His warm, brotherly way instantly made Hannah feel grateful he was here. Maybe he was a nice guy. Just maybe.

———

Hannah felt a bit more human after showering, but still weak. She knew she should eat something, but her queasy stomach shut down that thought as quickly as it came. She dried off with one of her mother's large, stiff towels, then used the damp cloth to wipe the steam off the mirror. Her face looked beaten; dried blood was still caked in her nostrils, and her nose was red and definitely swollen. She was afraid to touch it. *Did I break it?* she wondered. She scanned her body, turning around in the mirror and looking under and behind her limbs. The skin on her left hip had bloomed a shade of purple, and her ribs hurt when she breathed and moved a certain way. *This can't be happening*, she thought.

She could hear Deacon dragging chairs around in the kitchen, then the rustling of the large lawn bag she'd given him. Now he was moving the kitchen table.

She quickly dressed in sweats and went to help him. He had already cleaned up a good part of the mess. The linoleum floor just needed some mopping to remove the evidence of blood and some other type of gunk that was smeared across it.

The shattered sliding glass door posed the bigger problem. Together, they taped a few large garbage bags around the doorway to alleviate some of the chill. It was something Hannah thought her dad would do.

The idea of them coming home renewed her anxiety. She checked the wall clock: 11:00 a.m. Okay, she still had a few hours, but she needed to work fast, especially on her story, just in case Gamma Mimi sent them home early complaining about one of her convenient headaches.

Her grandmother and her mom didn't get along, and they barely spoke outside of these semi-annual visits. A headache excuse from either one of them usually signaled her family's impending exit, often to Hannah's relief. She didn't like the woman very much; Gamma Mimi was bitter and caustic, and showed her little affection. Mostly, Hannah stayed hidden behind her hair during visits there, avoiding her grandmother's judgmental gaze on her acne-ridden face, which was inevitably followed by a disapproving cluck of the tongue. Hannah could only imagine what she had done to her dad growing up.

The kitchen looked nearly back to normal when Hannah finally got up the nerve to ask him. "So how *long* have you been here?"

Deacon shrugged and continued sweeping. "Friday night, just a couple of hours. I went home in between to make an appearance. My parental units hit some fundraiser Friday night and slept in most of Saturday. Probably hung over. Next night . . . some charity benefit, same deal, different day," he said without meeting her eyes.

That's right, Hannah thought. Deacon's dad was some type of politician, running for office again—lieutenant governor or something. She'd seen his campaign banners around town. Tall and distinguished, Kingsley Giroux was a very handsome man. It was probably where Deacon got his dreamy good looks. His mom was an old society beauty too, in a regal, arm-candy kind of way. The town revered the Giroux family to some extent; they were local celebrities. Many were jealous, of course. They lived in a huge English Tudor in the nice part of town. Not much was said about their kids, though. Hannah had never crossed paths with Deacon before this week, except from afar at school. She thought he might have an older brother somewhere.

Hannah searched his face when he spoke about his family, detecting a touch of sadness in his voice, but like a light switch, Deacon changed his demeanor and smiled brightly— *a candy cane smile*, Hannah thought—before continuing his account. The moment strangely disarmed her, and something swirled around in her chest.

"I heard you fall inside, so I broke the sliding door. Looks like you smashed your schnoz pretty well, missy. Found you in the bathroom, just lying there not moving. I didn't know what to do. It was kind of creepy. But I could tell you weren't *dead*, which was a relief."

"Gee, thanks."

He shook his head, ignoring her sarcasm and glanced up at the kitchen clock for confirmation. "Could tell you were still breathing. So I carried you to your room and got some water. You slept for a long time. I went home to eat. Got nothing in this house, girl."

"So I've heard."

"Seriously, your parents left you to fend for yourself and didn't even leave anything in the fridge for you. Pretty bogus."

"Yeah, I'm so sure."

He looked at her and laughed. "You're pretty calm now after everything—"

"So what happened to me?"

Deacon met her eyes and took a deep breath. He closed them for a moment, exhaling before he spoke. "I didn't know what was up when I first got here. You just kept crying, really bugging out, screaming for your mom, your dad, to stop. It was like someone was hurting you, like badly. Geez, I've never seen someone get so fucked up." He paused and looked down at the broom he was leaning on. "You'd wake up for a bit and seem okay, but you were in a daze, just staring. I couldn't tell what you were looking at. And eventually you'd pass out again."

Hannah sensed Deacon studying her face. She looked away and could feel her face heating up. She hugged her arms, running her hands inside her sleeves, looking for small bumps on the back of her arms ready for picking and scratching, something to soothe her . . . but then she stopped, realizing he was still watching her.

"Bet you're pretty bruised up," he said—then, chuckling, he went on, "Dude, you pulled the kitchen phone out of the wall and just screamed into it. Dragging the cord all over the floor, crawling around with it, just weird. I kept yelling to you. That's when you ran somewhere and then boom, it sounded like you ran into the wall full speed or something. I broke the door to get inside and found you in the bathroom, blood everywhere . . . I almost blew chow myself."

"Oh my god," Hannah said. She began to remember bits and pieces of Friday night, but couldn't be sure what was real or imagined. Deacon's play-by-play was making her feel worse, like somehow she had failed at taking drugs for the first time. And *he* was the reason for what happened to her, with his "totally clutch" upsell, when all she had wanted to buy was some weed. The condescending smirk on his lips made her feel stupid and small.

"You f-ing son of a bitch!" she screamed and attempted to punch him in the face. Her fist just caught the edge of his jaw.

"Hey, *bite me*, Zandana! I was the one who took care of you. Cleaned up your mess in the bathroom, carried you to bed. Forget you!" he said, holding his cheek and stepping back. He glared at her, his brows furrowing like before.

"Go screw yourself; I could have died. What did you *give* me, anyway?" Hannah yelled.

"Just what you asked for. You came to me, remember?"

"You made it sound so chill. It was supposed to be your 'choice, trippy kind of stuff'—*remember that, Deacon?*—oh, and your 'zero aftereffect' bull? I could have died. Shoot, I think I had a seizure, bit my tongue and everything!"

"You didn't have a seizure. I was there remember?" he said, regaining his composure. He turned his back on her and reached for his coat.

"What did you give me, Deacon?"

"LSD, princess. What did you think?"

"I . . . I took LSD?" Hannah asked incredulously. She had never done something so reckless. And for what, to be cool in front of those girls who never even liked her? Thinking of them made her boil inside; it *had* been her idea to approach Deacon. And she'd done it just to impress them. *Stupid. Stupid*. She grabbed Deacon's arm.

"Hey, I'm sorry . . . it was just so frightening. It was the scariest, ugliest thing I've ever experienced. Like a gruesome, never-ending nightmare . . . *Twilight Zone* meets *Children of the Corn* . . . I can't get it out of my head. It really messed me up. I'm never doing drugs again. God, I swear. Never again."

CHAPTER 9

LOOKING DOWN INTO HER EYES NOW, THOSE STRANGE, captivating pools of emerald, for a moment Deacon forgot to breathe. Something inside of him shifted as he tried to swallow the acerbic taste in his mouth that had first appeared when he saw her on her basement floor and knew it was because of him. He never meant to deal her something she couldn't handle. He felt like a creep. He wanted her to be okay, and he wanted to stop feeling the guilt that had been gnawing at him since Friday night, when he thought she'd never wake up. He pushed away the thought and tried to make her, and especially himself, forget.

"Congratulations, you are now an honorary member of First Lady Nancy Reagan's 'Just Say No to Drugs Campaign!'" he teased in his best politician voice. Hannah laughed, and he liked the sound of it. Then, out of nowhere, she hugged him. Deacon's hands remained at his sides. He let himself inhale the sweet smell of her shampooed hair; the moist curls tickled his chin. Her body felt soft and warm against his, and oddly comfortable.

Cautiously, his hands made their way to her shoulders. *I should pull away*, he told himself, but he left them there a little longer. Half-heartedly, he patted her arms like he'd seen his father do when the cameras were around, signaling that the photo op was over. But Hannah held on. And he couldn't help it, she felt good. His hands found her upper back. His arms circled her body, pulling her closer. In that moment, he saw his father again, this time from long ago, embracing another woman—who was not his mother.

———

Deacon was playing on the lawn next to his house the day the sun, its cruelty timed perfectly, disappeared behind the clouds and opened his four-year-old eyes to what was happening on the other side of the living room window. He gaped as he saw his mother strike his father. He'd heard his parents argue before, but nothing like this.

He'd heard the name Brenda—or "cheap whore," as his mother referred to her—surface several times over the past few months. She was his father's campaign secretary, always at his side and on the road with him since his political career's grassroots beginning. Many said that their relationship resembled a dance—unspoken and beautiful, every step anticipated and eagerly received. A natural match, it seemed.

Deacon secretly loved seeing Brenda whenever he visited his father at his campaign office. She was always very patient and kind to him, playing silly games—so unlike his own mother. Sometimes he even pretended that his father was married to Brenda; many a night, he created fantastical dreams of the kind of life they'd have before crying himself to sleep over his real mother's indifference toward him.

Even at four, he knew that his parents' marriage wasn't

based on love or genuine affection, but money. His mother's father, Pierre Charbonneau, was an extraordinarily wealthy man who'd earned his fortune in plastics, the kind that went into faces, breasts, and other unmentionables. Pierre liked the politically ambitious Kingsley and his hardworking, right-wing sensibility, and hoped the young man could tame his wild, booze-loving daughter.

Babette had apparently grown up to be a handful, wild just like her own mother, who killed herself one night by jumping from the penthouse suite at the Waldorf Astoria while Babette, still a baby, lay nestled asleep.

Pierre didn't have much use for a daughter. His parade of girlfriends, along with his expanding business, kept him busy, so he hired a fleet of revolving nannies—none of whom did anything to lessen Babette's selfish temper. She grew into an ill-mannered, spoiled debutante. Deacon heard his grandfather say many times between his teeth, "Babette grew up beautiful, ungrateful, and *wicked*."

Two years after watching his mother hit his father through the window, Deacon sat in a drafty, chauffeured town car, brimming with excitement.

"Daddy's going to be so excited to see us, I know it!" He beamed up at his pretty mother; her expression remained impassive, but Deacon didn't care or try to contain himself. Finally they were surprising his father at work, something Deacon had begged for for weeks. His father's long hours on the road and extended weekends away from the family left a hole in his chest he couldn't quite understand. He especially missed Brenda, who he hadn't seen in months.

"Daddy's been working really hard, huh, Mother?" he

said, watching out the window, not expecting an answer. He sang quietly, entertaining himself with some of the silly songs he and Brenda used to make up together. He sat as still as he could, but inside his head bounced with thoughts of all of the many things he and his father were going to do that day. Maybe his mother would let him stay at the campaign office by himself, something he hadn't done in a while. He looked over at her to ask, but thought better of it.

When they arrived, he skipped up the short block to his father's campaign office. A young man held the door for them, giving his mother a shy smile as she went past. She didn't bother to acknowledge his presence.

A couple of steps in and Deacon suddenly smashed into his mother's leg. Babette sharply drew in a breath, her face unreadable. His own stomach dropped at the sight of his father holding up another young boy about his age. His father's face appeared warm, almost loving. Something struck Deacon's chest from the inside.

"Who is he, Mother?" he asked, but his mother pretended not to hear him. She just yanked his arm and walked him briskly back to the waiting car.

Two days later, Babette moved out, taking Deacon and her fortune with her.

CHAPTER 10

"I KEEP TELLING YOU, I DON'T KNOW EXACTLY WHAT TIME the robber got into the house. Sometime after midnight, after I went to bed. Geez, you don't even care that someone broke in when I was home alone!"

As expected, within minutes of their arrival home, Hannah's parents had flipped over the state of the sliding door. She tried to hold it together, knowing she'd lose them if she started to cry. Smug, six-year-old Kerry stood like an obedient soldier next to their mother, who gently stroked the little girl's head.

"I was really scared Mom . . . Dad," she said, looking into their faces for any hint of concern for her. "I hid for a while. When I didn't hear any noise in the house I ran to the bathroom, and that's when I must have fainted. I hit my nose on the sink, see?"

"Just go to your room, Hannah," her father said. Her mother said nothing, just absentmindedly played with one of Kerry's braids.

Hannah knew they didn't give a crap about her; what else could explain their lackluster response to her weekend nightmare? Somehow, her being safe after an intruder invaded their home was not the ending they had hoped for. What if she hadn't woken up from taking the LSD—what then? Would they have cared?

She walked slowly to her room, her bruised body and aching nose still demanding cautious movement. The familiar letdown from her parents' apathy slid into her chest like a blade. She was too tired to cry. She gave in to the pain traveling down her arms and into her thumbs and cuddled her oversized hippo to sleep.

The sleeping pill she'd lifted from her mother's wine cabinet before her parents got home had helped Hannah rest most of the night—except when she rolled onto her bruised side, which woke her multiple times—but she still slept through her alarm for school. When she woke up and saw the time, she closed her eyes again. *I'm never going to make it anyway*, she told herself. There was too little time to get ready and catch the bus. Besides, her body warranted other plans; it felt heavy and tethered to the bed. She could only imagine what her nose looked like. She gently rolled onto her other side and drifted back to sleep.

She woke again when the kitchen phone started ringing.

"Hannah? Well of course she went to school. Hang on—" Her mom dragged the phone to Hannah's room, holding the receiver to her shoulder. Hannah pretended to still be asleep.

"Okay, she overslept. I'll run her right over. Bye now," her mother said in her best singsong parental voice and hung up. Suddenly, she was back in Hannah's doorway.

"Get up! You missed the bus!" Her voice had lost all the

friendliness it had held during the phone call. "Get up, Hannah! I have to pick up my prescription from Dr. Falso's office today before they break for lunch. As is, I barely have time to *drive you*."

Hannah winced at the mid-morning sun streaming through the window. She looked over at her mother, still standing in her doorway with her hands on her hips. She was dressed in her new tweed blazer with the large shoulder pads, the perfect power suit for the stay-at-home mom.

"Mom, my nose. I can't breathe. I think it's broken. Please, I can't go to school," Hannah croaked. She couldn't remember the last time her mother had set foot in her room. Even now, she held on to the doorframe like it marked the edge of a quarantine area, impatiently tapping one of her heels and studying her Fossil watch.

"Sleep it off. I'll be back by noon, after I get your sister from school." She marched back down the hallway without waiting for a response. Hannah heard the jangle of her keys and the snap of her purse before the front door slammed.

She exhaled, relieved to be free for a few hours and not at school facing those evil girls—especially Gillian, who had lied to Deacon about her being away. But she wanted to avoid Deacon most of all. Not only had she feebly attempted to punch him, she had hugged him like a child before he left with his "duffel bag of evidence," the one filled with her incriminating bloodstained clothes and a few rags that wouldn't get clean.

She pulled a section of her hair across her lips, still thinking about him. She told herself he was just covering his own butt helping her. There was nothing between them; how could she believe for one minute that he, an incredibly handsome senior, would ever be interested in her, a pimply-faced sophomore?

She cringed at the thought of the whole school talking about her. She was sure those girls had spread multiple rumors about her by now. *Hannah took LSD. Hannah's a druggie! Didn't show up for school, jumped out a window, she's probably dead!* If only she had someone she could talk to besides her diary, not only about the nightmare that nearly killed her but the strange reality of Deacon spending the weekend at her house. It was all too weird.

She must have dozed off at some point, because she awoke to the sound of the kitchen phone ringing again. Probably her mother, she thought, and let it go. But the voice on the answering machine was nothing like her mother's.

"Ah, yeah, this is Officer Stevenson from the 16th Precinct. You asked me to check on all phone calls coming and going to your home this past weekend. We came up with nothing, Mr. Zandana. No calls were made to our station or 911. Thank you and have a good day."

She felt sick. Her parents were checking her story; they didn't believe her. She *did* call 911 Friday night, more than once. She'd genuinely thought there was an intruder, and in fact there had been—except it was her drug dealer coming to check on her. But they didn't know that. *Screw them*, she thought, steaming inside. If they *really* knew what had happened to her, would they have even cared? *No*, she thought, *it's all about that damn sliding glass door and finding out who broke it.*

She had to get out of her house before she went crazy.

She pulled back her knotted bedhead into a ponytail, slipped on her sweats, and walked out to the front porch. She closed her eyes, resting her hands on the railing, and inhaled the sweet scent of the fall trees still holding on to their leaves. The crisp wind circled around her neck like a scarf, creeping into her sweatshirt. She lifted her face to the autumn sun and was just thinking of going inside to get something to eat when someone called her name.

"Hannah!"

Her eyes snapped open wide, afraid to turn in his direction. *Oh no, my face.* She just woke up; she must look awful. Her skin. He couldn't see her without her makeup.

"There you are . . . guess you're alive after all," Deacon said.

Still not looking at him, she tried to make a mad dash inside.

"Hey wait, don't go . . ."

"I-I I got to do something . . ." She ducked her head in the doorway and sneaked a look back at him.

"Just wait a minute, will you?" he said impatiently, walking faster toward her.

"Deacon . . . I can't . . . I don't . . . please, don't see me like this." Her voice sounded like a child's, but she couldn't help it. No one, absolutely no one, ever saw her face natural and unmasked. She panicked at the thought of him seeing what she really looked like. *Oh my god, he just can't.* She couldn't bear it.

"You look fine, Zandana. Really," he said softly as he walked closer, stopping just below the porch steps and gazing up at her.

"W-What?"

"You heard me," he said with a small smile.

Hannah tried to act cool and relaxed about the fact that he was at her house again, while inside her heart spun in a constant rotation of backflips. All at once, she didn't know where to put her hands or how to stand upright.

"Did *you* ditch school?" she said after a moment.

"Sort of. I showed up. Then left."

And came here, apparently, she thought, but all she could manage to stutter out was, "W-w-why?" She hated the way her words got stuck when she was nervous. *God, he's beautiful*, she thought. He was looking up at her with his hands casually stuck in his pockets of his trench coat, wearing black jeans with his combat boots this time. Way cooler than Hannah's lame, frumpy gray sweats and dusty house socks. She pressed her lips together, tasting her wretched morning breath. And—oh god—she didn't have a bra on either. Her nipples must be hard as rocks. She self-consciously crossed her arms and shifted her weight onto her left foot, placing the other one on top.

His smile grew wider. "Well, you're alive."

"Yeah, I stayed home, not feeling great, and my nose . . ."

"It's less swollen, looks a bit crooked."

Shaking her head, she said, "Yeah, my mom is going to take me to the doctor when she gets home."

"When's that?"

"Soon . . . ahh, come in the house, I'm getting cold out here."

Deacon followed her and closed the front door behind him. He reached for Hannah's hand and turned her around slowly, bringing her inside his arms. She immediately felt a wave of protectiveness, his dark mystique enveloping her all at once and making her self-consciousness fade.

She closed her eyes and buried her face in his leather jacket. He smelled like an intoxicating mix of spicy vanilla and Drakkar Noir. She rested her head upon his chest, and this time their bodies pressed together. She knew her nipples were definitely hard now, but at the same time she didn't want him to try anything. She hesitated, feeling scared. He pulled back and tilted up her head, cradling the side of her face. Hannah shuddered at the sensation. It had been a long time since someone had touched her skin. She worried what he must think of her, especially her acne. She felt so exposed and naked under his gaze. But he just looked in her eyes and smiled.

"I like you like this," he said. Then he kissed her forehead gently, pulled away, and walked slowly out the door.

CHAPTER 11

"MO-OOM!" KERRY WHINED. "DID YOU GET ME MY LUCKY Charms, did ya, did ya?"

Hannah barely heard her little sister's words as she walked into the kitchen. She was freshly showered and feeling a little more human—and she was still on a high from Deacon's visit that morning, recalling his last words and how he'd looked at her. Utterly giddy, she kept repeating them to herself, sending her heart into flutters.

Her mother looked up from unloading her grocery bags and watched Hannah hand Kerry her box of cereal. "*You're looking better.*"

"I feel better, thanks. But Mom, my *nose* . . . I think it's broken. It's crooked, see?"

Her mother squinted from across the kitchen counter.

Hannah leaned over. "Look, it's not even straight. I can't go to school like this." *She won't even take me to the doctor*, Hannah thought, seeing her mother's skeptical expression.

"Humph," her mom managed after a moment. Then she looked tenderly at Kerry like Hannah wasn't even in the room. "Guess we'll be heading back out, my little one."

Kerry screwed up her face. "I don't want to go, I want to stay here and watch my show!"

Hannah made an immediate about-face and headed for her bedroom, not wanting to hear her sister's complaints. It was a joke how much they indulged her. *Such a brat; get a life.* Leaning against the inside of her door, she thought of Deacon again and smiled.

———

"Well, we can't fix her nose until the swelling is completely down," Dr. Kittleman repeated, his eyes fixated on the wall just past Hannah's shoulder. Her mom refolded her arms, appearing unsure where to look when the doctor addressed them. Dr. Kittleman was a diminutive man with squirrely eyes that were strangely magnified by his thick, foggy lenses. His peculiar pupils darted up and down when he spoke, but never met your face outside of a handshake—but even then, your forehead was as good as it got.

"Who knows," the doctor said with a nervous laugh, "maybe you'll like the way it looks."

Real funny, doc. Hannah scowled. *Who likes a crooked nose?* She wished she could kick the jerk.

"What about some pain medication for her, something to help her sleep? She's been complaining an awful lot," her mother said, to Hannah's great surprise. Wow, maybe the woman did care. It certainly hadn't seemed that way on the way over, which she'd filled with complaints about what an imposition this trip to the doctor's was on her day. Oh, and comments about how the family's health insurance was less than adequate to handle something like this, heaping on another layer of guilt.

"I suppose I could prescribe something," Dr. Kittleman said.

"How much will that cost?" Hannah's mom responded, her tone sharp.

Hannah sighed. Once again, she closed her eyes and imagined being with Deacon, the only good thing to come of this mess—almost worth getting in this much trouble.

CHAPTER 12

"I GOT YOU GIRLS STRAWBERRY HAAGEN DAZS," HER mother called from the kitchen, where she was unpacking grocery bags. Hannah winced; she thought she'd barf if she ever tried to eat that flavor again.

She looked over at Kerry who was thoroughly engrossed in her *Little House On The Prairie* episode. The sisters on the show, Laura and Mary, seemed so cute together in their earthy flowered dresses and bonnets—nothing at all like their relationship, Hannah thought. Maybe she should try harder. It would be nice to have someone on her side.

"So, Kerry, what's up?"

Hannah waited a few moments, but Kerry continued to ignore her.

"Yo, Kerry. Step away from the TV—"

"Shut up, you *muddafudder*, I hate you!" screamed Kerry, scrunching her nose so tightly the wrinkles obliterated her freckles.

Hannah was less amused at Kerry's mispronunciation and more shocked that words like that had come from her little sister's mouth. *Where in the world did she learn that?* Someone had snatched her cute sister and turned her into a monster.

"Listen Kerry, you can't talk to me like that."

"Why not? I just did, stupid."

Holy moly, what had gotten into her sweet baby sister? Hannah's nose began to throb along with her irritation. Kerry, meanwhile, went back to her show like nothing had happened.

Hannah got up to find her pain meds, but the new bottle was already half empty. That's weird; she'd only taken two so far. Hannah walked back to her sister.

"Get your feet off the couch," she said calmly, and swung her little sister's legs to the floor.

Like Drew Barrymore in the movie *Firestarter*, Kerry turned to her with the deadest, creepiest, possessed eyes, opened her mouth so she resembled a hungry baby bird, and screamed, "Heeeeeeelp meeeeeeeee, Mommmmy! Hannah's hurting me! Stop it, Hannah! Stop it! Stop hurting me. Heeeeeeeelp!!!!" The intolerable pitch of her shrieking sent Hannah's brain reeling.

Oh my god, shut up . . . shut this little thing up! She jumped off the couch just as her mother came barreling into the room.

"What did *you do* to your sister?" Her mother's pitchfork stare made Hannah back away before her mom scooped Kerry into her arms. Lovingly, she began stroking the little girl's hair. "It's okay, darling," she said softly.

The sight of them together made Hannah's stomach unclench, a sourness rose up the back of her throat. *Why her and not me, Momma,* she cried inside. The palpable love between her sister and mother hit Hannah like a blow; she couldn't catch her breath. One by one, the kitchen walls started to vibrate and crowd in on her. She took off and slammed her bedroom door behind her. Her feet slid out from underneath her; the bed caught her before she hit the floor. She wrapped her arms around her legs, rocking herself, until a familiar rush of hollowness carved through every cell and she grew numb from the exquisite pain.

It happened in a strange house, on an overcast rainy morning when she was six: she fell hard off a bed she'd been playing on with other children, ones she'd just met. Hannah's mother sat concentrating over a pile of papers at some lady's dining room table, along with the other mothers. What started as a silent cry turned quickly into a full-blown howl. Hannah's mouth splayed opened, blood drops appeared down the smocking of her dress. Her face contorted in the hurt and shock of the fall; it was the first time she'd had the wind knocked out of her.

She became immediately afraid in the unfamiliar house, full of kids who just stared, some pointing. Hannah ran to her mother, trailed by another little girl who stood there holding her ears.

"Momma!" Hannah cried, relieved to have found her. Believing comfort was in sight, she threw her body over her mother's carefully crossed legs, but someone pushed on her shoulder and she suddenly found herself on the floor, treated like an animal begging for scraps. Startled, Hannah looked up to see only the wave of her mother's hand, her signal that she was too busy for her now.

A mother's loving touch, that's all she wanted—to be

pulled into her mother's arms. But her mother never touched her in that way, and never had. It was Hannah's job to pull herself together and swallow the pain—and, in this case, the blood in her mouth. Around her parents, crying was not permitted, and any form of childlike "carrying on" was not tolerated. But for Kerry, it seemed, the rules were dramatically different.

CHAPTER 13

SHE'D MISSED THREE DAYS OF SCHOOL NOW, MOSTLY
wallowing in bed and watching TV when her sister was out
with her mother. (Ever since Kerry's last spaz-out on the
couch, Hannah had been avoiding her like she had AIDS.)
But Hannah couldn't take another bored minute being home.
Eventually, she knew she was going to have to face the inevitable drama at school and the whispers behind her back, and
she was unsure how it would all go down.

That morning, she slowly made her trek to the bus
stop—her mother, of course, had refused to drive her to
school—with a pit growing in her stomach. She'd wanted to
call Deacon for a ride but was afraid he might laugh. "Two
house calls for the newbie drug-taker and that's it," she imagined him saying. And yet she'd still mustered up the courage
to call him—only to discover his number was unlisted. Figured. *Just as well*, she thought. They hadn't spoken since his
surprise visit on Monday, and Hannah wondered what he was
thinking, especially about her.

She skipped her usual make-up mastery, mostly because
her lovely nasal passages were packed in gauze and deeply
yellowed on the outside around the bridge of her nose from

slimy Dr. Kittleman shifting her nose back in place. It had hurt like hell despite the topical he'd given her, licking his lips before securing the bridge of her nose between his sausage fingers and, in one swift motion, repositioning it. The sound alone, like the crack of a batter's bat, nearly made her cry. She'd immediately felt sick and lightheaded—something about an issue of equilibrium when dealing with the nose area, he said. Whatever it was, Hannah nearly hurled up her breakfast right there in his office while her mother waited in the car.

One positive to come out of her ordeal were her pain meds; what little were left in the original bottle seemed to help her acne. Or maybe it was just that she was too tired to pick at her face, as her tender nose kept waking her up at night, robbing her of sleep.

So, despite the circles under her eyes, Hannah left her house the most "natural" she'd been in years, with just mascara, eye liner, and some Bonnie Bell Lip Smacker over her crusty lips. And it felt good to be less made-up for once—until she spied the three of them at the bus stop, standing there in their designer jeans and crewneck sweaters, obnoxiously gaping at her.

Their laughter made Hannah alter her path and head toward one of the peripheral kids circling the coven. Peter, was it? She gave him a small smile, trying to be nonchalant and ignore them, but she heard every word.

"Oh my god, just look at her nose! Looks like she got into a fight. Total Scarebear. Fugly, fer sure," Gillian screeched spectacularly in attempt to entertain the crowd.

"Yeah, why is she even here? I wouldn't be caught dead

going to school like that," Leeza chimed in—adding, with her best Valley Girl movie voice, "I'm so suuuuuure!"

"She's like Rocky Balboa," Gillian continued, egging her friends on.

All the peripheral kids snickered.

"Pa-the-tic," Taylor said in her most snooty, condescending voice.

"Shut the *F* up!" The words came out faster than Hannah's brain could stop them. She caught the shocked looks from the peripheral kids as she turned around. It was now or never. "*Bite me.* No one cares what *you* think," she said, getting right up in Taylor's face, the easiest target of the three. Her eyes ablaze, she clenched her right hand, ready to hit Taylor's pretty, perfect little nose. "Just one more word out of you . . . you . . . *slut!*"

Gillian and Leeza looked stunned. Taylor's eyes started to well up.

Hannah stepped back, surprised at herself. She felt bad for making her cry.

"Whoa! Hold on there!" someone called out as Hannah stood there shaking, the adrenaline making her body feel warm and alive. Gillian and Leeza had already backed away from Taylor, leaving her vulnerable for the kill. *Such loyal friends*, Hannah thought.

The voice came closer. "Stay away from my daughter! Hannah, what in the world has gotten into you? Taylor honey, are you okay? Why are you girls fighting? . . . It's okay, honey." Taylor's mom crooned in an exaggerated motherly tone, putting her arm around her sixteen-year-old daughter's shoulder and walking her toward their house. Taylor was really crying now, and her mother looked back and gave Hannah her best evil eye.

Good, one down. Hannah didn't feel bad anymore. Her juices still pumping, she readied herself for whatever the other two had next for her—but the sound of the bus interrupted the exchange. Everyone headed toward its open door in silence. Gillian and Leeza climbed on faster than normal and walked briskly to the back. Hannah plopped down in the front seat next to Peter. He slid closer to the window, and she suddenly felt spent.

Hannah had barely spoken to her seatmate before today, due to her preoccupation with the coven in the back. He was a tall, sort of quiet kid. She had noticed that he sported a different concert T-shirt, carefully tucked into his jeans, every day. His favorite bands seemed to be Depeche Mode and The Cure, as evidenced by the Robert Smith tee he was wearing today. Hannah looked at him briefly, out of the corner of her eye. He wore his dark blond hair parted down the middle and feathered to either side, the ends just skimming his shoulders.

The bus ride seemed quieter than usual, except for the driver's radio announcing the "high of the day" before kicking into another twanging country song. Hannah stared straight ahead all the way to school, as did Peter—but just as the bus pulled into its parking spot, she noticed him glancing sideways at her. A small smile crossed his lips, and then he said, "Nice going."

"Ah . . . thanks," Hannah said, surprised he was talking to her, let alone complimenting her. Well, at least she had a fan. God, she knew that it was a crazy thing to do. And going after Taylor may have been a bit unfair; she probably had the best relationship with her out of the three. Of course, that was why Taylor didn't see it coming. And even though she wasn't the ringleader and was basically civil to Hannah on her own, Taylor was still a mean girl, Hannah reasoned—one that had to be stopped.

Hannah turned to get off the bus, but couldn't help stealing a glimpse at Gillian and Leeza in the back first. The two appeared deep in conversation.

A breeze washed over her face, lifting up her hair, as she stepped off the bus into the parking lot. Lightheaded, and feeling a little sick over what girl-trouble could be headed her way, Hannah found herself looking for him.

"Zandana." He was right there, leaning against her bus with Toby at his side. He immediately approached her, appearing amazingly handsome as he left the jock abruptly once again. "Hey, how's the schnoz? You look a little freaked out."

Hannah fidgeted with her book bag, still unnerved by his gaze. He tilted his head, watching her. Gosh, he was charming. *But why is he being so nice?*

Deacon shook his head, smiling. "Come on," he said, and he slung his arm around her shoulders and began walking her into school. Hannah felt her back melt at his touch, her clenched jaw replaced by a plastered-on smile that gave everything away. He was like a calming drug. Just knowing that he'd been waiting for her made her want to pinch herself.

"Hey, don't worry about these losers," he whispered in her ear as they walked toward her locker. "They're just a bunch of doofuses."

Hannah laughed at his word choice and tried to ignore the onslaught of stares and dropping jaws in their path.

"So are you still checking up on me?" she said. The words came out with a gasp, and she realized she'd forgotten to breathe for the past couple of minutes. "Seriously, your services go above and beyond the typical dealer's," she said, trying to sound like she knew what she was talking about.

"Always, Zandana. I want my customers *satisfied*," Deacon said in a devilish tone, and he smiled a smile that reached his eyes.

The moment ended as quickly as it started when his beeper started going off in his coat pocket. He pulled it out and grimaced. "Ah, I got to take this. Catch you later?"

Hannah nodded, but she felt a stab of dread creep into her chest as he walked down the hall, taking with him her armor. She sighed and looked back into her locker, numbly staring at the shelf brimming with textbooks and spirals, trying to remember where she was.

Suddenly, Gillian was at her side. "That little tirade is going to cost you!" she hissed in her face, forcing Hannah to recoil.

Gillian sped away without looking back, but her venom hung in the air. Hannah tried to shake off the chill running up her neck. Gillian looked like she was out for blood. Hannah chewed her bottom lip, blinking back her wet lashes. The bell sounded. She grabbed her books and quickly headed to class.

———

Her classmates' eyes popped wide open when she entered English, just like they had in her other classes. Hannah ducked getting to her seat, avoiding their stares and wishing that her desk would swallow her up. Her packed nose ached and a headache had claimed the space between her eyes, brought on by the unsettling energy around her. The other kids' questioning looks and whispers only got worse as she pulled on the ends of her hair, wrapping them tightly across her lips like a shield.

Finally, Mrs. Myers appeared, and Hannah could exhale. *Get this day over with*, she thought.

"Well, Hannah, I see you've returned to us," Mrs. Myers said, peering over her glasses. "I presume you completed the assignments while you were home *sick.*" The emphasis she placed on that last word caught Hannah's attention, and she searched her teacher's face. Apparently everyone knew something had gone down over the weekend, something that caused her to break her nose and stay out of school. Hannah could only guess what people had made up to fill in the blanks.

"No, m-ma'am, I didn't have the assignments."

The class chuckled; they, like Hannah, knew what was coming next.

"You didn't call one of your classmates for the missing work?"

"No. I wasn't feeling well," Hannah replied, focusing her gaze on the greasy head of the kid sitting in front of her and wishing Mrs. Myers would cut her some slack.

"Hannah, see me after class," the teacher said briskly.

Hannah did her best to feign interest in the adventures of *Madame Bovary* for the rest of class, but she could barely follow the discussion and longed to be back in bed, hiding under her comforter. She dawdled in her seat after the bell sounded, slowly packing up her stuff to evade any more attention. She knew what they were thinking: *Hannah, you freak.*

"Hannah," called Mrs. Myers, her heels clicking toward Hannah's desk in short, rhythmic strides. The steely look in her teacher's eyes made her slink back into her seat.

Uh-oh.

CHAPTER 14

———————

"COME HANG OUTSIDE WITH ME," DEACON SAID, SUR-prising her at her locker, where she was crouched down filling her book bag to go home. Her heart lifted at the sight of him and his puppy-dog eyes with their long lashes. It had been a long and strange first day back, and she just wanted to get out of there. Then again, avoiding Gillian and Leeza on the bus ride home and getting to spend a little time with Deacon did sound enticing.

She stood up facing him. "Okay, for a little bit; then I need to get home."

Deacon's smile gave her heart another tiny jolt. He took her hand for the first time as they walked outside together to the open space behind the school. His hand felt warm and strong, and above all surreal.

She wondered where they were going. She didn't play sports and only ventured to the back of the school during gym—her most embarrassing class, and the one she most dreaded, due to her innate lack of coordination.

The backside of the school consisted mainly of cracked slabs of blacktop with a couple of picnic tables that were a known hangout for smokers—or "Heads," as they were re-ferred to. On any given day, Heads could be seen wearing a

Mexican serape pullover in a multitude of colors, their hair all greasy and wild, humming Grateful Dead tunes and usually cutting class.

There was one school payphone outside. Some of the kids used to use its phone number as their home number, so when the school secretary or a teacher wanted to check why a student was late or absent from school, his or her friend would be conveniently outside to answer it and act like the parent. Hannah had heard it was a great scam until too many kids tried it.

The surrounding fields including an outdoor track, soccer, and football stadium lay empty awaiting afterschool practices. Deacon steered her to the table nearest the payphone and casually sat on top of it with his forearms resting on his thighs. Hannah took a spot next to him, pretending it was the most natural thing in the world, hoping they'd actually have something to talk about to take her mind off wanting him to kiss her.

"I should call my parents . . . tell them I'm going to be late," Hannah said hopping off the table. She felt Deacon's eyes on her, which made her ears grow hot. She found a quarter in her bag and dialed home, but there was no answer. *Figures*, she thought, and returned to Deacon, who was staring at her and smiling.

"What?"

"Does it still hurt . . . a lot?" he asked, rubbing his palms slowly together, which for some reason she found distracting.

"My nose? Yeah, but only if I accidentally hit it. Still tender," she said, and she self-consciously touched her nose to test it. But she could tell that Deacon was focused on something else. His eyes darted to either side and behind him as two pimply-faced kids approached, both wearing stone-washed jeans and Izods with the collars up. *Good grief* she thought, *they're only freshmen—band kids even.* Hannah watched one of them nervously extend his hand. Deacon shook it while keeping his eyes steadily on the two of them before he in one motion slipped the kid's ten-dollar bill into his pocket and pulled out a small bag. He cupped it in his hand with his palm facing the ground and covered the boy's hand again with his own to complete the exchange. It all happened so quickly that before Hannah knew it, the two young boys were off again without so much as a word.

Hannah watched them walking away and shifted her position on the table uncomfortably. Until recently, she'd had no idea this even went on at school. She looked back to read Deacon's face. "So this is what you do? Sit out here and wait for *customers?*"

"Yep. They come to me. No reason to get pushy or draw attention . . . plus, it's safer here than on the streets or in the park. Less chance of getting jumped."

"So, do you do drugs too . . . like, a lot?"

Deacon laughed. "Not usually. Just an occasional toke from a batch of weed . . . you know, to be sure what I'm selling is good and worth the *moola.* Quality control, baby," he said in his car salesman voice.

Hannah tried to wrinkle up her nose, but it ended up as more of a sniff. "Do some kids die . . . you know, from the drugs?"

"Overdoses are bad for business," Deacon said matter-of-factly.

Hannah felt her throat catch. "Guess I would have been your first . . ."

"Don't," he said grabbing her hand. "I don't want to think about it. I fucked up. Sold you more than you could handle. That's not how I do things." He looked away, releasing her hand.

"So, you feel bad, is that it?" Hannah said wrapping her arms around her legs. She could feel a heaviness inside her chest pushing her into the ground, yet still she needed to hear it.

"Yeah, I feel bad," Deacon said quietly. "Especially since I like you."

CHAPTER 15

"TAYLOR'S MOM CALLED TODAY. SHE SAID YOU *ATTACKED* her daughter at the bus stop?"

Her mother started her inquiry as soon as Hannah walked through the door, looking like a TV reporter from the comfort of her corduroy couch.

It was well after 6:00 p.m., and Deacon had just dropped her off. She still felt high from hanging with him after school, then riding in his car; she couldn't wait to write it all down in her diary to relive it. They hadn't said much on the drive home, except for shared sidelong glances that seemed funny at the time, like a private joke between them.

He'd held her hand as he drove, too, and squeezed it just before she got out of the car. Their eyes met for what felt like a long time when they said good night. The moment was straight out of a movie, and Hannah thought she'd die right there. She was still floating in dreamland when her mother stopped her.

The rest of the house was dark and the makings of any sort of dinner nonexistent. Hannah just wanted to crash and think about Deacon. But her mom persisted.

"Hannah, what in the world? I don't need to be getting a phone call like that."

"What's this?" her dad said, walking into the room. He picked up his newspaper and settled into his recliner.

"Nothing," said Hannah, and started to head to her room.

"Not so fast. Hannah got into some kind of scuffle with Taylor, the girl up the street. Her mom called me today. Taylor ended up staying home, she was so upset."

Big dip, Hannah thought. *She deserved it.*

"First the glass door and now this?" Her father's voice was already rising. "You're turning into some sort of hoodlum, and I won't allow it!"

Hannah nearly laughed out loud. *Hoodlum?* "That's right, Dad, I broke into our house even though I know the garage code," she said, unable to control herself. "And now I'm beating up the local tramp!"

Hannah and her father glared at one another, neither one flinching as the kitchen clock knocked off each unbearable second. Her father's face went from a slow simmer to a full boil before she could even blink.

"Just go to your room, you're grounded! No kid talks to *me* like that."

Hannah started to her room then changed her mind. "I'm tired of *you* yelling at *me* for every little thing! You never believe a word I say. You have the cops checking my story. And you haven't a clue what those girls have done to me since we were kids! You two are the worst. Mom's stealing my pain meds and your almighty righteousness—" Hannah realized her mouth was dispensing information faster than her brain could censor it. Her father stopped and looked at his wife, who suddenly sat up straighter.

"Is that true, Donna?"

Her mother's features froze like a statue. Then she blinked.

Her father shook his head. "Forget I asked! That's just another damn lie out of your mouth. Now go to your room and stay there!"

———

Hannah woke sometime after 9:00 p.m., feeling out of sorts and more than just a little hungry. Her clothes were damp, like she'd broken a fever in her sleep. She listened for sounds coming from the kitchen before venturing out, wondering where everyone was.

Just the light above the stove was illuminated; the rest of the house sat still. With a peanut butter sandwich in one hand and a glass of milk in a plastic McDonald's Hamburglar cup in the other, she shuffled back to her room in her house socks and old sweats, where she eased herself onto her bedroom floor. She sat cross-legged with her back against the bed and took a bite of her sandwich, sensing a long night ahead.

Two hours later, after trying to make some headway on the schoolwork she'd missed, Hannah climbed into bed, eagerly welcoming the notion of sleep, when she heard a small noise. She rolled over, ignoring it, but it persisted—a tapping sound with an inconsistent rhythm. *No wind does that*, she thought. She stood on the bed for a better look, and that's when she saw him.

Oh my god, they're going to freak, I'm so dead, she thought, panicking. She had to get rid of him. Slowly, she opened her window, praying it wasn't going to make that screeching noise it usually did and wake everyone upstairs. The crisp

October air rushed into her face, sending harsh chills down the inside of her sweatshirt. The smell of burning wood filled her nostrils as she whispered frantically into the darkness, "What are you *doing?*"

"Gonna let me in?" Deacon asked, standing below her window, his hands resting in his coat pockets. He shivered slightly as his breath made white puffs in the night air.

"No way! My parents' window is just above mine. They'll *totally* hear you."

"Come on, let me in. It's cold out here," he whispered back, looking up at her with those irresistible puppy-dog eyes, a persuasive trait of his that Hannah was beginning to recognize as deliberate. It still made her smile.

She could tell he was standing in her mother's hydrangea bush—a skeleton now, barren of leaves, but wickedly sharp. Her windowsill was eight feet from the ground; he'd need something to stand on in order to clear it. She grabbed the step stool from her closet and handed it down to him. As soon as he stepped on, it immediately sank into the ground. He repositioned it on the bush, most certainly damaging it, but it did the trick: he hoisted himself up and climbed through her window.

Hannah's heart stopped as they clasped hands, teetering together on the bed, listening intently for any sound coming from upstairs. After a moment, she exhaled. Deacon stepped off her bed and let his trench coat drop to the floor. He lay back on her pillows and motioned for her to join him, but she shook her head and sat at the edge of the bed, straining to hear anything outside her room, her brain screaming that they were about to get caught.

Deacon made himself at home, resting both hands be-hind his head as he crossed his feet and watched her. The moon outside was bright enough that even with the lights off, she could see his face.

"So, hi . . ." she began uncertainly.

"Hi," he said softly. "Surprised?"

Hannah nodded. "Kind of." Her heart flipped wildly out of her chest, not knowing if it was out of exhilaration or fear that he was actually in her bedroom. As her eyes slowly adjusted to the darkness, his features became crisper. "So . . . *why?*"

"My parents were out, I didn't want to be alone."

"You're crazy, we totally could get caught."

"Probably." With that, he reached for her hand and turned it over, tenderly kissing her palm. His lips, cold against her skin, sent a tingly sensation down the inside of her forearm like an electrical current. She didn't move her hand, wanting him to kiss it again. His lips brushed the inside of her wrist, igniting more vibrations down into her elbow. Hannah cupped his cold cheek, transferring her warmth to him. She became transfixed by the angles of his face, wanting to run her fingers along every turn and slope.

He broke the spell by pulling her toward him. Shyly, she leaned into him, and he wrapped his arm around her. She started to calm down a bit and relaxed her head onto his shoulder. They didn't speak for a few minutes, and Hannah wondered if he had fallen asleep. She picked up her head slightly and saw him staring somewhere beyond her closet. She felt grateful for the shadows cloaking her tiny room, along with her stuffed hippo, which lay facedown in the corner.

"Do your parents stay out a lot?"

"Yeah, they're never home. Yours?"

"I wish." Hannah inhaled, enjoying the subtle remnants of his cologne and wondering if he wore the same one every day.

"Are they over the sliding door yet?"

"Hardly."

"Parents suck."

Hannah nodded absently, watching his chest create waves as he breathed. His body took up most of her bed.

"Did they ground you?"

"Yeah . . . not like I go anywhere, though," Hannah admitted, thinking that she probably sounded like a dork.

"I'm out all the time," Deacon said dryly.

"With friends?"

"No . . . work. Sometimes at parties, mostly to deal. People always want something." His voice drifted off like he needed her to ask him more. Instead, she bit her bottom lip, unsure what to say and trying not to think about that side of him. She didn't even know where he got his drugs or if he'd ever gotten busted. *Why would such a gorgeous, well-off boy resort to dealing?* she wondered.

They both got quiet, listening to the night outside. Hannah decided to let the mystery of Deacon remain for now, and to simply relish in the fact that he told her today that he liked her. Part of her still found it hard to believe, but then again he'd just snuck into her bedroom, which was probably the wildest and dangerous thing that had ever happened to her—except for accidentally taking LSD of course.

"You're beautiful, Hannah. Those eyes . . ."

She flushed. "It's dark, you can't possibly see them."

"I noticed them the first time . . . and every time after. They're like peacock feathers: green, gold, sort of a purplish-blue. They keep changing, like a kaleidoscope."

"It's my built-in mood ring," she said loudly.

"Shhh, you want them to catch us?" Deacon said playfully, and turned her toward him. He brushed back her hair a couple of times, then tilted her face up to his and kissed her—once, then again, sending a strange sensation through her and down below. Her smile gave her away and she kissed him back, careful not to hit her nose. *Oh my god, I'm kissing Deacon Giroux*, her brain squealed in delight. The frosty air lingered on his lips, but his tongue tasted warm and delicious, with a hint of mint.

He pulled away slowly, smiling. "Mmm, peanut butter."

Hannah's hand flew over her mouth, and she cursed herself for not brushing her teeth before bed.

"My favorite," he said, moving her hand away and kissing her again.

———

Just as the sky started to lighten, Deacon lifted himself up. He gazed into Hannah's eyes for a moment and gently kissed her forehead, before jumping down from the window. Hannah again prayed he wouldn't wake anyone. She watched his dark form cross over the next two neighbors' lawns, growing smaller by the second. Still, she could see it when he pulled his coat around him tighter, and his breath was still visible. She fell back onto her bed when she finally heard his car start; her sheets still held his scent.

She drifted off almost as soon as she closed her eyes—thoroughly exhausted, but for the first time, blissfully at peace.

CHAPTER 16

Her alarm blasted her back into reality. She slammed it down and didn't look back.

"Hannah, get up!" her mother yelled from the kitchen.

Twenty minutes later, she threw her legs over the side of the bed—and only then noticed the streaks of mud on her windowsill, down her wall, and across her sheets.

"Holy . . ." Quickly, she stripped the bed and stuffed the evidence into her closet. She frantically wiped down her window and wall with a sock and threw it in as well, just before her mother threw open her door.

"I'm up, Mom. Ready to go."

"Hurry up. I'll drive you."

"Think I just witnessed a miracle," Hannah muttered under her breath.

"What?"

"Nothing. Thanks, Mom. I'll be right out." Hannah dressed like the house was on fire, pausing only to splash cold water on her face and hesitating for a millisecond in front of the mirror. *The natural look will have to do*, she told herself. Screw her father and his tirades over her acne. Then she thought about seeing Deacon and hastily applied some eye-liner and blush. Still, she couldn't shake the feeling she was forgetting something.

"Hannah!"

She made it to school as homeroom was ending. She could barely keep her eyes open. She spied Deacon down the hallway, talking to someone she didn't recognize, as she grabbed her books from her locker. When she looked back again, he was gone.

She fumbled with her lock, swearing underneath her breath, and scrambled to class with everyone else. She was used to being invisible, but today for some reason she wasn't. *God*, she thought, *is my sweater on backward or something?* Hannah glanced back and caught some students looking at her weirdly. She tucked her head into her binder, holding it tightly against her chest, and soldiered on through the crowd. She heard her name as she passed the cafeteria. To her right, a boy stood laughing with a group of jocks. They all looked up and stared. *Now what?* she wondered, shaking her head. Rumors spread so quickly at school . . . *Oh my god. Gillian.*

The redheaded witch had told her that she was going to make her pay. The thought made Hannah want to cry. All at once her legs grew heavy and thick, each step becoming more unbearable than the next. Where could she hide now? Maybe she should beeline it for the nurse's office and claim really bad cramps. More laughter erupted behind her. *Come on Hannah, pull it together, it's nothing*, she told herself, *nothing at all.* She began tugging on her hair, pulling the strands tight around her lips. *God, now I have more enemies in this school without even trying.*

She prayed that she was imagining the strange shift around her. She thought about Deacon, and wondered if he knew if anything was up. Why did people twist everything she did? Sometimes they judged her before she even opened her mouth. *Just a few more feet to first period, you can make it,* her brain coaxed. Her thumbs now tingled, and her eyes were inches from tears as she entered her classroom, not meeting any of the kids' faces.

Push it down; push it back down.

―――――

Mrs. Myers kept calling on her again in English, probably to keep her awake. Sitting there, Hannah felt strung out from lack of sleep. Her thoughts kept drifting to her mother finding her closet filled with the evidence of Deacon's nighttime visit; she wondered if she could get home in time to wash her sheets without her noticing.

Her life had gotten so complicated in less than a week now that Deacon was in it. He seemed so daring and willing to take chances. It was exhilarating to be with him. When he kissed her, he made her feel beautiful. His seductive presence coursed through her veins like a drug, and she found herself wanting more.

Hannah sprang up to leave as soon as the bell sounded. She had to find Deacon to see if he knew anything. She heard a couple girls laughing behind her and looked back to see if it was about her. But then Peter from her bus stepped in the path of the two girls, stopping them in their tracks.

"Shut the F up," he said, glaring at them, before turning to look directly at Hannah. His liquid blue-hazel eyes flashed her a message she didn't understand. Embarrassed, she quickly walked away. *What the hell was that about?*

Hannah dawdled at her locker between periods, wishing she could ditch school altogether. She shook her head; something was off, big time. She closed her locker and turned around—and came face to face with her worst nightmare. The coven was blocking her from going in either direction, with Gillian perched proudly in front, her cold, cobalt eyes seeping venom. Leeza stood in second command with her hands on her hips, wearing her newest preppy cable sweater and kilt pin skirt—looking no more threatening than a Girl Scout on cookie delivery night. Taylor, on Hannah's left, couldn't even make eye contact. Her bored stance made it clear that she didn't want to be there.

Like magic, kids filled in behind them, rubbernecking and jamming the hallway. This attack had been announced. Panic seized Hannah's throat, preventing her from swallowing. Her eyes darted around the growing mob. *Where's Deacon, where the hell is he?*

"Yeah, keep on looking. This time your *boyfriend* isn't around to help you," Gillian sneered. Hannah could almost see blood dripping from her canines.

Hannah closed her eyes, trying to remember the words Mrs. Myers had preached to her the previous day. Towering over Hannah's desk, the young teacher's resolve had oozed of spitfire and sass—but also kindness. Distracted by her teacher's sudden change in demeanor, Hannah hadn't quite heard her the first time, causing Mrs. Myers to repeat herself.

"You are better than them. Smarter. *Braver.* Stop getting in your own way. Believe in yourself. You, Hannah Zandana, can be and do *anything.* They're afraid of *you.* Now act like it. *Go.*"

"I think she fell asleep," Gillian said, and the other girls laughed. Hannah heard another kid behind them yell something she couldn't make out.

What the hell am I going to do now? Then it came to her. *Scare them.*

Hannah lunged forward with everything she had, running her upper body into Gillian's and catching her off guard.

The redhead immediately stepped back a pace.

"You f-ing dyke," Hannah said in an angry whisper. "Get out of my face or I'll tell everyone what you are. You don't think I know about you?" Out of the corner of her eye, she could see the exchanges around her—the shaking of heads, the confused looks. Even Leeza gasped.

"Whaaat did she just say?" asked Taylor.

"Nothing . . . right, Gillian?" Hannah said, louder this time, as Gillian's eyes grew into saucers and her lower lip displayed the faintest of quivers. *Got her.*

"Nothing, she fucking said nothing," said Gillian. "Come on, this is bullshit. *She's* bullshit."

To Hannah's incredulous relief, the coven turned and single-filed it through the crowd as they parted for them. The onlookers disappointedly followed, leaving Hannah alone. She was left speechless, unable to fully comprehend what had just happened. *What the . . . ?*

She had guessed right.

CHAPTER 17

*D*ID *I* *ALWAYS* *KNOW?* HANNAH PONDERED THAT QUESTION the rest of the day. Probably not, but there were inklings—pieces she hadn't put together until today—like the games Gillian would orchestrate when they were kids, including those awful kissing ones. But nothing concrete until that night last July, when she saw something she shouldn't have.

Hannah's mom had sent her to retrieve her sister's ball from Gillian's yard—the one with the princess characters, Kerry's absolute favorite. Hannah heard voices near the back deck and looked over. Gillian's back was to Hannah, a dainty hand with dark polish grabbing her butt. She hadn't seen the girl before; she was very pretty, but not from their school. It was dark though. Hannah didn't think Gillian saw her—she was too involved in the kiss. But the other girl did; Hannah could tell by the way her eyes expanded in alarm then turned pleading.

Hannah clumsily scooped the ball into her arms and quickly got out of there.

———

"Heard you had a bit of drama today," Deacon said, slipping his hand into hers as they walked together through the parking lot to his car after school.

"Sort of," Hannah said. "I took care of it."

"Heard that too. What did you say to them?"

"Nothing, really."

The thought of Gillian liking girls was so foreign and completely unexpected, but then, everything about Gillian had always put her on edge. She realized now that she really didn't know Gillian at all, and few people, if any, probably did. Was it possible that behind Gillian's wicked persona was a misfit just like her? Maybe that's why she worked so hard at ganging up on people—to gain power and control over them so they couldn't do it to her first. *Who knows*, Hannah thought. She felt naïve when it came to girls liking girls. No one ever talked about such a thing at school. But she knew all too well what it was like to have secrets no one else could understand. How exhausting it was.

They got into the car, and Deacon smiled at her and rested his hand on her upper thigh—something he'd never done before. Hannah began to chew on the ends of her hair, but quickly stopped when she saw him watching her. She continued to tug on her hair, however, as they drove. With Depeche Mode playing in the background, she thought about Gillian and the girls taking the bus home when they passed the houses into her neighborhood. She wondered what Monday would bring, then pushed the thought away and smiled at her "boyfriend," as Gillian had referred to him. Hannah wasn't even sure Deacon considered them to be "going out." *What* are *we doing?*

Deacon pulled up to Hannah's house. Her mother's station wagon was parked in the driveway.

"I'd have you in, but . . ."

"Oh, I have my ways," he said in his devilish tone.

"You sure do," she said, grinning. "I'm exhausted. Did you sleep any?"

"Nope," he said. His eyes narrowed, and he nodded toward the driveway. "I think someone is sleeping in your parents' car."

"What?"

But Deacon had already jumped out and was heading toward the station wagon.

"Deacon, what are you doing?" she said, following him, scrambling to keep up with his long strides.

"Could be somebody trying to steal it . . ." He stopped diagonally behind the driver's side window then looked back to Hannah. "It's some woman."

"M-Mom . . . what are you doing in the car, are you sleeping?" She tried the door. "Mom, unlock the door!"

Her mother blinked several times. "H-hannah . . . you'rrre home earrrrly," she said after her second fumbling attempt to open the driver's side door proved successful. She stood on rubbery legs, making slow and deliberate movements, her eyes bloodshot like she'd been crying.

"I got a ride. Mom, what are you doing out here . . . where's Kerry?"

"Inside . . . watching TV." She swallowed, but it sounded more like a burp. "Ooh, 'scuse me . . . I must have dozed off . . ." She held on to the side of the car.

Hannah looked back at Deacon, wishing she could read his thoughts, but he was already looking away, his hands jammed into his pockets.

With much effort, her mother straightened her body and

pushed herself away from the car. Finally, she noticed Deacon off to the side. "Who are *you?*"

"Deacon, Hannah's friend," he replied, reaching his hand out. But instead of shaking it, her mother used it to steady herself as she stepped past him and walked warily back to the house.

When she was safely inside, Hannah looked at Deacon. "I've never seen my mother drunk before—"

"She wasn't."

"Huh? What do you mean?"

"Her pupils were huge."

"What does *that* mean?"

"Nothing." Deacon shrugged. "Forget it."

"I . . . I should check on my sister."

"That's cool. Wanna go to the movies tonight? There's that new Talking Heads movie, or maybe we could see *Thief of Hearts* . . . or *Crimes of Passion?*"

"I think you're on a roll there," she said with a laugh.

Deacon grinned. "So what time should I get you?"

"I'm still grounded," she said and sighed, her fingers busily twirling strands of hair as she crossed her other arm underneath her elbow.

Deacon's beeper went off. "One sec," he said, glancing down. When he saw the telephone number, his jaw tightened.

"What?"

"Nothing, just can't stand this guy . . . I may need to shake him loose."

"Why . . . ahh, never mind, it's none of my business," Hannah said.

Deacon reached out, took both of her hands, and draped

them around his waist. He clasped his own arms around Hannah's back and began to kiss her. His lips felt silky against hers. Hannah felt his warm tongue enter her mouth. She moved her body to touch his and it set off a delicious storm of tingling sensations ripping through the front of her. Reflexively, she pulled him closer—but then she remembered they were standing in front of her house. Suddenly self-conscious, she thought about her mother and pulled away.

"Sometimes I can't believe you're here with me," she said breathlessly, unable to look into his eyes. "I met you a week ago and it still feels so . . . surreal."

"I can't believe I never noticed *you* before."

"I can," she said, screwing up her face like he was crazy.

"No really, you're so cool and easy to be with . . . mature, too, not like other girls . . . *and* you use big words like 'surreal.'"

Hannah laughed. "Seriously, you can date anyone you want in the school, maybe you already have—"

"I don't date."

"What?"

"I don't date."

"Then what are we?"

"I like you," he said and gently cupped the side of her face. This time she leaned into his palm and closed her eyes, letting the electricity from his hand run through her.

Abruptly, his beeper went off again, awakening her back to reality. Hannah watched him walk over to his car. He came back holding her book bag.

"I still want to hang with you," he said, his chocolate-brown eyes conveying a different meaning as he slid the strap of her bag over her shoulder.

"Sure," she assured him, trying to sound nonchalant though her stomach twisted slightly as she wondered how she was going to get out of being grounded.

"Call you later," he said. He glanced back at her house and lowered his head to kiss her again. Then, with another look at his beeper, he got into his car and started the ignition, giving her a quick wave before peeling out.

Hannah stood outside until his car disappeared into a small dot. Her heart felt full, yet sad at the same time, and it had everything to do with him. *So this is what it feels like*, she thought.

She took a deep breath before opening the front door. She closed her eyes, letting herself enjoy the magical moment a little longer. Then she stepped into the place where the pain lived.

"Come here, Hannah," her mother said in a weak voice, her legs propped up on the arm of the corduroy couch in the living room. Though she looked and sounded beat, her mother's words came out fighting.

"That display you put on in the driveway made you look cheap."

"Mom, we're just friends."

"A boy like that is going to give you a reputation."

"Better than what I have now," Hannah muttered under her breath.

"What did you say?"

"Nothing . . . he just gave me a ride home."

"Who is he, anyway?"

"Nobody."

"Nobody wants to be with you?"

"Basically," Hannah said. She heard the TV in the other room. "Kerry okay?"

"Of course she is," her mother replied, her tone unmistakably indignant.

"She's only six, Mom."

"What the *hell* does that mean?"

"No surprise, my parents won't let me go to the movies tonight," Hannah told Deacon later that evening, sitting cross-legged on her bedroom floor and twirling the phone cord around her fingers. "Guess it's *Friday Night Videos* again for me."

"Nah, let's talk some more, I've got time."

"Where are you?"

"Home."

"But I called your beeper."

"Yeah . . . you can call my other number . . . it's separate from my parents'."

"Okay. Wow, your own number. Impressive."

"Not really," Deacon said, sounding distracted.

"I would love that—" Hannah heard his beeper going off and she knew she'd lost him. "Deacon?"

"Later tonight, okay?" he said as he hung up.

Hannah curled her legs into her chest and rested her head on her knees, feeling bored and lonely all at once. She squinted at the stains on the carpet from her LSD trip, remembering how she thought she was going to die that weekend. If only she had a girlfriend or an older sibling to talk with about all the strange and exciting things happening to

her—someone to help her navigate the beautiful yet dangerous enigma in her life that was Deacon.

Hannah cautiously touched the sides of her nose as she
rose to peer into her mirror. It definitely felt better, and most
of the yellowing had gone away. She smiled, thinking about
what he said about her eyes and how she was different from
other girls; she'd never realized that could be an asset. Deacon was pretty different than most boys Hannah knew at
school too, and he was undeniably gorgeous—everyone could
see that. *But why me?* He was two years older; maybe he
didn't know what a loser she was in her grade. She shook her
head. None of the boys paid any attention to her, and the
ones who did acted like jerks, snickering and calling out her
name to make fun of her. It had been like that for as long as
she could remember.

"Why *not* me?" she told the girl staring back at her with
her hands on her hips, but she only got an eye roll in response. Chagrined, she headed to her closet and began to
primp for her "date." Late night bedroom rendezvous would
have to do for now.

Hours later she lay in bed bored, rereading the same page
in her *Seventeen* magazine on how to apply makeup before
school in less than four minutes. The dimple-faced model on
the page sported short, bouncy hair, nothing like Hannah's
untamable abundance, and naturally she didn't have her
abominable skin. Why did these types of magazines always
leave her feeling worse about herself? *Thanks for the subscrip-
tion, Mom, but it doesn't seem to be working.*

She pushed the magazine aside, wishing she had a good
book to read. Her neck felt stiff from not moving. She'd

spent an hour on her makeup, and ever since she'd been lying on the bed like Snow White awaiting her prince, her hair carefully splayed atop her pillow.

A pair of headlights danced across her window. She immediately froze. Then she heard a car idling outside her house, and she felt her pulse go into overdrive. She glanced at her clock: 11:34. She jumped on top of her bed and craned her neck to see what she could, pressing her face against the window, but the car passed; it was nothing, yet again. Hannah felt her nose twitch as she turned off her bedside table light and pulled her comforter up to her chin. She listened and waited, wishing he'd get here already.

Any possibility of sleeping in, even for a Saturday, was greatly reduced with Hannah's curtains open. She'd left them that way all night, hoping Deacon would show, and now the sun was infiltrating her small room with all its force. Reluctantly, she lifted her face off the pillow then fell back down again, burying it further. It took a couple of times to crack open her mascara-glued eyelashes. She blinked away the gunk smeared across her contacts. Her eyes and skin itched from sleeping in her makeup, a fact that had been recorded by her pillowcase.

She flipped her pillow over to hide the black stains, then rolled onto her back—still fully dressed, her bra feeling two sizes too small.

She thought about Deacon and started to worry. It was too early to call. She closed her eyes, but not to sleep; tears trickled down her cheeks and into her ears. As always, she felt like a fool.

CHAPTER 18

———

"Hey."

"What happened to you?" Hannah tried to sound casual, but the question came out more accusatory than she'd wanted. She had avoided taking a shower all morning, not wanting to miss his call. Her diary had received the bulk of her rant as her brain rehearsed several smart responses she'd give him for standing her up, but at the sound of his voice, all of her pluckiness dissolved.

"It got too late," he said, his voice sounding groggy. Hannah pictured him still in bed. "Sorry . . ."

"It's okay," she replied, her fingernails absentmindedly scraping some of the makeup from the previous night off her cheek.

"Can I swing by and get you?"

"My parents are home, probably not."

"Tell them you need to study at the library and I'll pick you up there."

———

Hannah saw Deacon's car parked around the corner as she hopped out of her parents' station wagon. She was grateful that her little sister had a birthday party that afternoon, a convenient fact that had distracted her mom from asking her too many questions. Hannah hardly ever asked to go to the library to study, preferring the solitude of her bedroom to the cliquey study groups she always found there, composed of the same classmates she dodged during the week. Saturday afternoon, though, she figured it would be pretty empty. And besides, she wasn't planning on staying there for long.

"I have to stop at the drug store later today," her mom yelled to her as Hannah climbed out of the car, ignoring the faces Kerry was making at her from the backseat. "Have any quarters to call?"

Hannah nodded without looking back, hustling toward the library's large double glass doors. When she entered, she stopped just before the checkout area, looking around for him.

The first floor resembled a ghost town: just a few kids and their parents. She had just walked past the elevator and was heading toward one of the rectangular study tables near the windows when someone grabbed her shoulder and pulled her into a small hallway. His exuberance startled her. Before she knew what was happening, he pressed his mouth down on hers, leaving her gasping.

"Hi, you look great."

"So do you," she said, letting his dazzling smile wash over her. He smelled really good as he wrapped his arms around her, too. It felt like a dream to Hannah, to be so wanted.

"I missed you."

Deacon opened the passenger door for Hannah and gave her a quick kiss before she got in. His attention never left the white Buick parked in the corner of the lot with the engine running. He couldn't tell if they were the same two undercover cops from last night—the ones who stopped him on some bullshit charge. He still felt lucky they'd let him go, though the whole thing left him unsettled; to hassle him then release him wasn't what cops did in his town. But then again, Deacon had a feeling that they weren't from around here.

Feeling shaken, he had waited out the rest of the night parked between two cars on Hannah's block, catching glimpses of her looking out her window. Seeing her calmed him, so he'd just sat and watched her.

Now his instincts told him that a decision would have to be made in the next minute or so. He purposely wasn't holding today, which was definitely the right call. *But why are those two back again?*

"Are you hungry?" he asked, maneuvering his rearview mirror to give himself a better look. He grabbed Hannah's hand and kissed her fingers before gunning it out of the parking lot.

———

He steered Hannah to the back of the diner, where they could be alone and he could still see the front entrance. Only then did he relax a bit. He still didn't have much of an appetite.

He watched her dip each French fry in her gravy with a delicate determination he found fascinating. Her lips strangely captivated him, as did her sensual neck when she swallowed. He licked his lips, making her blush—something she seemed to do a lot.

"I used to come here as a kid with my dad . . . a long time ago," she said quietly, glancing around. "Hasn't changed much."

"Were you close then?"

"Sort of." Hannah stopped eating and pushed her plate aside. "What about you, are you close with your parents?"

"Hardly. They do their own thing . . . I do mine."

"They give you a lot of freedom, it seems. I'd love that. Mine are super strict."

"Mine aren't around much, too busy campaigning. It's more of a strategic marriage."

"They didn't marry for love?"

"No . . . not love," he said, letting the last word linger on his tongue as he reached across the table for her hands. "Brrrr, cold," he said, making her smile. "What about you? Ever been . . . in *love?*"

"I don't—maybe," she said, shifting in her chair and avoiding his eyes.

"I can see how the boys would fall for you. Getting lost in those eyes. They look green now with what you're wearing."

"Hazel."

"So pretty. And that wild hair," he said, sliding his chair closer to her to run his hand through it. "So cool how it springs back when you pull it." He chuckled slightly, rolling her curls between his fingers.

"I hate it," she said, but she didn't pull away. Her Irish skin reddened further, but he could feel her hand warming up to his and see her body beginning to relax.

He leaned all the way across the table. "I don't, I think it's cool . . . different," he whispered in her ear just before kissing her neck. Hannah squirmed like it tickled, then turned her face to his.

"You like that?" he teased. She nodded shyly. He gave her the kiss that she wanted, but then he went for her neck again, this time not letting her get away.

CHAPTER 19

Maybe there was a temporary truce going on. Neither Gillian nor Leeza paid any attention to Hannah at the bus stop on Monday morning. All the worry that had built up in her shoulders while she got ready for school slowly melted away. Quietly, she thanked God for small favors. If knowing Gillian's secret ensured her some peace, she was more than happy to take it—and she couldn't help but feel a little bit powerful, too.

"Hi," she said enthusiastically as she plopped down next to Peter on the bus.

"Hi, yourself. Good weekend?"

"Very."

"Ready for our quiz in Mrs. Myers's?"

"Ahh . . . guess I forgot."

"You'll probably ace it anyway, she likes you."

"Not when I missed her class last week," Hannah said, rolling her eyes. She looked past Peter out the window and noticed it was beginning to rain.

"How did you break your nose, anyway?" he asked after a moment.

"Long story." She watched the water droplets on the

window a row ahead of them elongate into thin streaks, changing form the more the bus picked up speed.

"It had something to do with that guy, Deacon, didn't it?"

Hannah shook her head no, but could feel her ears getting hot.

"I saw you that day in the hallway with him. He sold to you, right?"

"No . . . he didn't," she said, yanking on pieces of her hair. Peter's liquid eyes made her turn away. She started to get up out of her seat, throwing her book bag over her shoulder and swinging her legs out to the aisle, but they were still blocks away from school.

"Hannah, I . . ." Peter's hand gently touched the sleeve of her jean jacket. She looked down at her forearm; his fingers were long and honey-colored, like the rest of him. "He's not a good guy. You should be careful."

───────

Getting off the bus, Hannah did her best to shake off Peter's comments. She could feel his eyes on her, and she nearly stumbled off the last step. Around her, the rain had stopped, replaced by the fall sun threading through the clouds, making her wish she'd worn her sunglasses. She inhaled one of her favorite smells: that sweet, earthy scent after a long-awaited rain, when the world seemed saturated in color and clean for a brief moment. But even that didn't lift the sour taste in her mouth.

Hannah searched through the throngs of kids loitering outside, knowing she'd feel better once she saw him. She frowned when she realized he was with that same jock again but approached them with a cordial grin, wondering why Deacon hadn't introduced them to one another yet.

"Hi, I'm Toby," the guy said without a hint of warmth when she reached them, his eyes dissecting every inch of her. She felt instantly uncomfortable.

"Hannah."

"Catch you later, bro?" Toby said as he slapped Deacon on the back, sliding his hand across it. He didn't wait for an answer before walking away.

Hannah squinted at him as he left. He was like a jittery child, checking out people to either side of him and self-consciously running his hand through his auburn hair.

"What's *his* deal?" Hannah asked.

"Nothing . . . just a poser."

"Why do you hang with him then?"

"I don't, he finds me," Deacon said darkly, but then his face brightened and he pulled her to him, tilting her body from side to side. "You look great," he said before he dropped his chin to kiss her. "Mmmm, you sure we need to go to school?"

"*I* definitely do," she said, laughing. Deacon sighed, giving in, and draped his arm around her before wheeling her around toward the school entrance. Hannah let her hand inch slowly around his waist, finding her rhythm as they walked in together.

"There's a Halloween party on Saturday, wanna go?"

"I have to see," she said excitedly. "I'd like to go . . . it's just my parents . . ."

He kissed the side of her head. "I'll break you out if I have to."

Saturday night, Hannah opened her front door and jumped back at the sight of a towering, black-cloaked person on her doorstep, his face shielded from the porch light inside an ominous hood.

"Grim Reaper?" she said after a beat.

Deacon laughed and gave her a kiss. "Where's your costume?"

"I can't go . . . I called you a bunch of times, but there was no answer."

"Shit, okay." He leaned close and whispered, "I've got an idea."

Her arms shaking and her stomach wrung in knots, Hannah dropped, mid-prayer, from her windowsill to the accompaniment of her parents' bedroom TV. The bottom of her jeans caught on the hydrangea bush and sent her tumbling to the ground. She lay paralyzed for several seconds, staring up at the window and listening for any movement from their room, but just the light from the TV flickered back.

She had been careful to close her bedroom curtain behind her before she jumped, but any hint of wind would still give her away if her parents opened her bedroom door. All of the numerous ways she could get caught, including that one, ran through her head as adrenaline thumped through her ears. Hannah searched the cold grass for her cat ears, which she'd managed to find in the attic without her parents noticing. She'd dressed in all black and turned the tip of her nose into an upside-down triangle, complete with symmetrical whiskers. Not bad for a last-minute costume.

At last, she found the ears. She held her breath and cut across the neighbor's lawn, then began walking quickly, avoiding the glow from the street lamps. She could see him in his car about a block away. The motor was running, and his frosty breath made it look like he was smoking.

"Deacon, I'm so frickin' scared . . . what if they come down and check on me?" she whispered frantically as she slid into the car.

"Come on, we're late."

Hannah could hear the party before they even pulled up to the house. They were definitely on Deacon's side of town, where every palatial abode seemed bigger than the last. Hannah sighed, taking in the mansion—every light holding its own through an array of majestic windows and reminding her of a lit Christmas tree. *Gosh it's gorgeous*, she thought, wondering what it would be like to live among so many rooms and wander around in designer clothes and perfectly coiffed hair and makeup, just like on *Dynasty*. How could you *not* be popular with a home like that?

The house was set back from the street on a slight hill that led to a wide circular driveway. Cars were parked everywhere, even on the lawn. Deacon pulled his car in backward, parking practically in the neighbor's yard.

"Whose house is this?"

"Some schmuck."

"Whaaat . . . why are we here, then?"

"I wanted to be with you tonight . . . besides, it's great people watching." Deacon chuckled and kissed her hand. "Be my girl?"

Hannah nodded, liking the sound of it. She waited as he walked around the front of the car to open her door. His cloak nearly reached the ground, making him seem even taller than normal—and more foreboding.

"I'll take good care of you. Just don't leave my side."

Cat ears in place and holding her breath, Hannah stepped through the massive double front doors, feeling every bit the party crasher who would soon be discovered and ceremoniously kicked out. She squeezed Deacon's hand, readying herself for the ejection.

Deacon strolled in with his chest lifted and shoulders back. He immediately acknowledged a few of the guys with a casual lift of the chin, and several kids called out his name. The party appeared well into full swing, based on the state of the house and the swarm of people already there. The whole school had apparently showed up—or at least, all the cool kids, including the jocks and cheerleaders, were there. Not a nerd was in sight. There were kids she recognized in orange *Ghostbuster* jumpsuits, and a couple in that *Beetlejuice* striped suit, complete with black eye circles. Some *Karate Kid* characters with rolled bandannas tied around their heads were partying together with rubber bracelet–wearing Madonnas and colorful Cyndi Laupers, straight off of MTV. Hannah's cat costume looked childlike in comparison.

Deacon held her hand and steered her through the crowd of sweaty bodies and drenched heads to the massive kitchen, and then out to the backyard deck, where the keg was. Hannah felt like she was with a rock star; she could almost taste what it was like to be popular. Her eyes grew wider at every turn as she soaked in her first high school party, realizing how much she'd been missing.

Deacon's cool expression, meanwhile, didn't waver. He pumped the keg a few times, filled two cups, and passed her one.

"What do you think?" he asked, looking bemusedly at the side of her head. He reached over and pulled a few twigs out of her hair.

Hannah smiled, bringing the plastic cup to her lips and letting the icy liquid strike her empty belly. "You know it's my first . . ." she said, shivering slightly.

"I figured . . . no big deal, you're not missing much. Keg parties are pretty much all the same."

"Do the cops usually come?"

"Shit, hope not. Then we'd really be screwed," he said, raising his furry eyebrows in alarm. He smirked and leaned in to kiss her, but stopped inches from her lips.

"What?" Hannah was confused.

"Nothing," he said, and he brought his mouth to hers, hesitating a little before pulling away and saying, "Come on, it's cold out here."

They could hear people talking loudly over the music when they passed the mansion's central hallway. It seemed filled with kids seeking refuge from Van Halen's *Jump*, which was blasting from the living room stereo. Hannah's head jerked back at the sight of Gillian and Leeza leaning against the wall, holding beers and talking to some tall kid dressed as Prince from *Purple Rain*, wearing a gold chain that showed off his sprinkle of chest hair. Gillian was dressed like one of the members of Duran Duran and blatantly flirting with the guy, while Leeza, wearing Princess Leia's slave costume from *Return of the Jedi*, was bobbing her head with a fixed smile like a marionette.

Gillian turned and gave Hannah an icy once-over before bellowing for all around to hear, "Look at the *skank* who just walked in."

Mortified, Hannah shrank back behind Deacon's shoulder and turned the other way.

"Look who's calling who a skank . . . the queen of skanks," Deacon threw back.

"Why the fuck did you bring her here?" sneered Gillian.

"Not your flavor, bitch?"

Hannah pulled on Deacon's arm, trying to get him to move away as Gillian's face grew ugly, her viper eyes slicing into Hannah.

"Come on, let's go, Deacon," Hannah pleaded. The guy in the Prince costume was moving toward them, and Hannah could feel her human ears prickle with heat.

"Dude, I'm supposed to yell at yous, but I kinda need some weed," he said in a thick New York accent; he was clearly not from their town. "Got any?"

"No," Deacon said, glaring at Gillian. "Come on." He walked Hannah back into the empty kitchen, where it was quieter.

"Do you know that guy?"

"Never saw him before. Could be a cop."

"Wow, really?"

"Don't be so impressed," he said, shaking his head. He

played with the light switches until just the ones above the stove and sink glowed.

A tall, skinny blond girl from one of Hannah's classes, dressed like the mermaid from *Splash*, entered through the back door with a guy in an Indiana Jones costume. Hannah was trying to place him when the girl dramatically flung herself toward Deacon like he was her long lost friend, tripping over her mermaid tail as she approached. Hannah gasped when she tried to kiss him. Deacon snapped his head back, dropped Hannah's hand, and pushed the girl away.

"You're loaded, Clarice," he said, appearing annoyed.

"Nooooooooo," the girl sang back gleefully. Her eyes were clearly glassy, and she bent toward his ear and gurgled something Hannah couldn't hear. When she pulled back, she noticed Hannah next to him. "Aren't you in my history class?"

Hannah shook her head. "Spanish."

The girl nodded sizing up Hannah, then looked back at Deacon. "Arrrrrre you two a couple?" Clarice hiccupped the last word. "That's uuuutterly convenient, get all the weeeeeeed you want . . . since when do you hook up, Deeeeeacon?"

"What do you want, Clarice?" he said impatiently.

"Dime bag, pleeease."

Deacon checked the bill she passed before reaching into his pocket, all the while surveying the three different entrances into the kitchen. Now Hannah understood why he had turned most of the lights off: he'd been setting up shop.

Another boy wearing a straggly black-haired wig and an AC/DC T-shirt approached them a moment later.

"Dude."

"Billy the acid king," Deacon said quietly to Hannah. "What do you need?"

"Same."

"Three-oh."

The rest of the night consisted of similar transactions, so many that Hannah lost track. Deacon had a nickname for almost everyone. She couldn't believe how many kids from her school liked to party like that—drinking and using, seeking out pot, cocaine, even acid. It seemed like Deacon carried an endless supply. The tall Prince guy with the gold chain walked back through the kitchen at one point and stopped in front of them.

"Got a light?"

Deacon shook his head and gave him a bored stare. The guy narrowed his eyes and turned to another couple who helped him light up his joint right there. All three of them took hits, holding the sweet smoke in their lungs until they couldn't stand it. He then offered Hannah a hit.

"No, not her," Deacon said sternly, putting his hand up to the guy's chest. The guy shrugged and walked out to the crowd hanging out around the keg.

"Are you protecting me or something?" Hannah asked. The idea of it felt sexy to her, but maybe that was the beer talking.

Deacon rolled her into his arms, his face suddenly serious. "I don't want you to . . . ever."

He kissed her one last time before they scrambled to the side of her house underneath her bedroom window, both of them trying not to laugh and make more noise than they already were. Swearing under his breath, Deacon successfully hoisted her up after the third try. Hannah cringed as she slid through her window and landed headfirst on her bed. Like a gymnast scoring a perfect ten in competition, she rose triumphant, beaming back down at Deacon below. She reached down, clasped his hand, and whispered good-bye before he headed back to his car.

Hannah carefully closed her window and flopped down on her bed, her heart bursting out of her chest as she listened in earnest for sounds above her room.

Her bedside clock was blinking, stuck at 1:35. The power must have gone out on her side of town, too. The music had abruptly cut off while they were at the party, and the house had gone dark. The kids' initial screams had soon turned into laughter and whistles. Just then, out of nowhere, Deacon grabbed Hannah and pulled her through the back door and down the deck stairs.

"Where are we going?"

"Just come, hurry."

Both out of breath, they quickly got into his car. Deacon released the parking break and let the vehicle glide down the lawn into the street without turning on its headlights.

"What is it?" she asked after he started the engine a few houses away. "Why are we sneaking off?"

"Sometimes the cops cut the power . . . anyway, we should get you home." He took her hand and kissed the inside of her palm. "Wish we could stay out all night together."

"I'd like that," she said, moving closer to him to rest her head on his shoulder. She thought about the parade of kids who had come up to them, some of them talking to her for the first time. She'd never spoken to so many people in her life. For Hannah, it felt nice to be noticed for once.

"Do you hang out with any of those people, the ones who came into the kitchen to buy?"

"Nope."

"Me neither," she said, yawning.

———

Hannah watched the sky outside her window, thinking about the wild and strange ride the whole night had been—all because of him. She couldn't believe she'd snuck out of her house and gotten away with it. At last she heard his car pull away—their "getaway car," the one carrying the dangerous boy she couldn't stop thinking about. Eventually, she fell asleep still wearing her cat ears and black whiskers, hoping for more magical nights like this one. She liked being "his girl."

CHAPTER 20

———————

THEY MET UP EVERY DAY BEFORE SCHOOL AND AFTER FINAL period. Hannah wasn't sure where Deacon went during the day, she rarely saw him between classes. Every morning she looked forward to walking with him into the building and through the halls, always with his arm wrapped around her waist, blissfully feeling like his and only his—and then, of course, kissing him by her locker before she headed to class. He called her most nights, too, usually after ten, but some times they only got to talk for a few minutes before he had to head out. Hannah wondered when he slept or ever did homework.

School was a lot more bearable with Deacon in her life. Hannah couldn't wait to see him every day. The way he looked at her, like she was the most important thing to him, made her feel strangely confident.

"You look beautiful," he told her one afternoon after school, leaning against the bay of lockers while she collected her notebooks and binder.

"You say that every day," she said, grinning up at him. It was true, he did, but she never tired of him telling her so. And she took extra care now in the mornings before school, getting up early to get her makeup and hair just right, sometimes even setting her wild tresses in Clairol Benders, those flexible heat curlers that always burned her fingertips. She'd wear them overnight to tame her hair into some sort of style, always hoping that he'd notice. Often he did say something, which she lapped up like a puppy.

"But you do," he said playfully.

"What if I told *you* that?" she teased, feeling bold.

"I'd say that you couldn't see me."

Hannah's stomach fell, and she froze, thinking the moment she feared was finally here. She searched his face. His constrained grin didn't match his words or the shot of sadness in his eyes.

"The real me," he finally added after a long, torturous pause—and like a light switch, his eyes brightened again, restoring her breath.

Hannah turned back to gather her books, letting the chill his words had made run up her back and settle, as his left hand absently played with one of her curls.

"Where do you want to go?" he asked when she climbed into his car Thursday after school. It was the day after Halloween, and Hannah had dragged herself through most of her classes after staying up late into the evening, waiting for him to come over. He'd never showed. He blamed it on it being an especially busy night for him—and, to Hannah's delight, he was being extra attentive and affectionate with her now. It made it almost worth getting stood up again.

Hannah just wanted to go home and take a nap. But the

look on his face melted any sort of conviction, as it had since she'd known him.

"Your house?"

"Probably not a good idea," he said.

"Guess mine, then."

Deacon threw her a mischievous look, making Hannah laugh.

"This time you can see it during the daytime."

"Ah, I think I already have missy . . . like, our first weekend together?"

"Oh yeah, that's right," she said. Had her LSD trip really happened a mere three weeks earlier? It seemed forever ago.

Deacon rested his free hand on her upper thigh while they listened to New Order, letting the music sweep the cares of the day behind them. When Hannah realized that she was biting the ends of her hair, she stopped, tucked the strands behind her ear, and placed her hand over his. They arrived in her neighborhood and to her surprise Deacon kept driving when they saw her mother's car in the driveway. For a minute, she thought about the embarrassing time they found her mother asleep outside in the car. She pushed the thought away and glanced over at Deacon. Something told her that she wasn't going home anytime soon.

Gossamer Park sprawled for nearly three hundred acres in the center of town around a manmade lake. It was surrounded by walking trails, a paddleboat area, and frequented fishing spots, and was home to the oldest trees in the area, with plenty of pavilions and picnic areas where teens and derelict old men liked to hang out—until the park patrol kicked them out, anyway. Growing up, local kids held their birthday parties there, which had made Hannah curious about the place, especially since she was never invited to one. Neither of her parents had ever frequented the park, not even to push Kerry in a stroller when she was a baby like other moms did. *Just another facet of their antisocial weirdness,* she reasoned.

Deacon swung his car around under a row of towering oak trees facing the lake, over which the autumn sun was slowly fading. He left the keys in the ignition to keep the heat on, jammed his hands in the pockets of his leather trench coat, and stared out over the water. Hannah shifted in her seat and pretended to take in the scenery, but after a while she felt puzzled by the growing silence; it was making her anxious. More than once, she spied Deacon's pensive profile out of the corner of her eye—the same face he'd had on when he'd talked to the Prince guy at the Halloween party. She stuffed her sweaty palms under her legs and waited.

Finally, she couldn't stand it any longer.

"What's up?" Her voice seemed small and strange to her ears.

Deacon looked like he wasn't going to answer, but after a few breaths he finally did, his gaze steady and unchanging like the water. "Ever wonder what it would be like to walk into the sun . . . literally out on top of the lake, sinking deeper and deeper, until you were completely under and all you could hear was the water, deadening all sound . . . until there was nothing?"

"Huh?"

Deacon rested his elbow on his door window and ran his fingertips over his face and eyelids. He pinched his bottom

lip between his thumb and forefinger. "I used to swim com-
petitively when I was a kid. It was the only place where I
could . . . you know, like, relax. Letting the water rush
through my ears . . . slicing it with my hands . . . taking it on
like it couldn't break me. Nothing could, least I thought so.
Every day, I couldn't wait to get back in the water, to escape
from all the noise, where it could just be me . . . at peace.
Alone."

"Do you still swim?"

"No." He let out a strange laugh. "I once told my parents
I made the high school swim team. And needed to go to
practice at school, early in the morning."

"But—"

"I know . . . the school doesn't have a pool. Now you
know how involved my parents are."

"Geez. Where do you go, then?"

"I don't sleep much, so I really do go to school early, but I
just hang out. I don't really tell people this, but I get a kick
out of watching the janitors." He looked over at Hannah. "I
know, weird. They smoke their red cartons of Marlboros together before work . . . stand around laughing . . . sharing inside jokes . . . patting one another on the back. They're like a
family, it's fascinating to watch," he said, smiling—but his
enthusiasm quickly extinguished itself. He pressed his lips
together and his gaze hardened once again.

Hannah looked out onto the water, then back at him. Not
knowing what to do, she placed her hand on his shoulder and
squeezed it.

"It's not like I'm in a rush to go home after school. I hang
out in the courtyard. Kids find me. If it's cold or crappy out-

side, I chill in the cafeteria . . . basically watching the janitors move trash, sweep shit up, mop, whatever. Their lives seem so easy and uncomplicated, simple." Deacon hesitated and intertwined his fingers with hers. "Every day, they get a chance at a fresh start." He looked over at her; he seemed more tired than she'd ever seen him.

"Don't your parents ask why you don't bring home any medals from swimming?"

"I guess they think I suck." He laughed darkly. "Most times, they don't even know when I leave the house."

Hannah's chest swirled with a familiar sadness that for once wasn't hers. Her body felt stiff, her legs prickly from sitting so long. She still had no idea what to say. They both watched as the last bit of sun got completely swallowed up by the lake. It was then that Hannah realized she'd never felt closer to anyone in her life. With a shy smile, she climbed onto Deacon's lap and nestled her head against shoulder. She could feel his heart beating against her body. He tightened his arms around her, protective and strong.

Without words, Deacon began kissing her, cupping her face in his hands. He ran his fingers through her hair, sending tingles down her scalp and the back of her neck. His breath quickened when his mouth plunged deeper into hers. She could tell he was getting excited, and it made her feel high. He suddenly pulled away and peered into her eyes, making her chest do backflips. She kissed him then, her lips traveling over his smooth, flawless face, the one that had become a tantalizing drug for her, tugging on her like nothing she'd experienced before. Instantly, she felt insatiable as an addict, unable to take her eyes off his godlike features. Overwhelmed, she closed them and waited for him to kiss her once more, but Deacon withheld until she looked at him again. When she did, he ran his hand along the front of her neck, forcing her to tilt back her head, exposing what he was after. He dove back into her, devouring her neck, his kisses escalating, holding her all the while to keep her from pulling away.

All at once, her body heat climbed and her coat and sweater became unbearable against her skin. Deacon helped her out of the jacket and then the sweater, maneuvering her around the steering wheel. His hand found her breast outside her blouse and stayed there. Hannah started unbuttoning his coat, suddenly wanting to inhale every part of him and press her lips against his sweet-smelling skin, starting with the warm spot between his neck and clavicle where his cologne lingered the longest.

They moved into the backseat. Deacon slipped out of his coat and kicked off his boots. Hannah had never seen him in just his black T-shirt and jeans and it startled her. She lay down on the bench seat and Deacon followed her, scanning the area outside the car before letting his body sink into hers. The weight of him sent heavenly chills down her spine, into her limbs, and through her fingers, electrifying her all at once.

"Oh, Hannah."

"It feels . . ." she whispered back.

"I know . . . so good," he said breathlessly into her ear, running his tongue along her neck until she let out a small moan. Hannah sheepishly buried her face until she saw him grinning. *So this is what it's like*, she thought, *to want someone, every part of him.* Her mind drifted into a dream world where it was just the two of them, alone together, forever in love.

Deacon pulled back. "Shh . . . do you hear that?" His eyes stopped on something beyond the window. Then Hannah heard it too: voices, and they were getting louder. Separate balls of light danced along the car's front side window, bouncing ominously through the fogged glass. *How long have they been there, were they watching us?* Hannah worried, biting her bottom lip, her eyes darting around wildly.

"Wait here," Deacon said. He casually straightened his clothes, then climbed over into the front seat to grab his coat and boots. Hannah blinked a few times watching him, but the tears still came streaming down her cheeks. She hid her face when he opened the driver's side door. When he slammed it shut, the whole car shook, along with her in it. Her arousal cooled, replaced by a sudden feeling of shame. Her parents' voices storming her head: *You slut. Whore. He's cheapening you.*

Lying low on the seat, she quickly tucked in her blouse and pulled on her sweater with shaking hands. Then she cleared the damp curls from her face—and that's when she heard them. Laughing. She tugged hard on the ends of her hair, grabbing fistfuls, straining to hear. *He's telling them,* she thought. She closed her eyes. Whatever they had just shared together, the closeness she had felt to him, both were long over.

Several moments passed and it felt like agony, but still Hannah couldn't make out what they were saying. It was dark and she knew she had to get home. Her parents would surely kill her for this one. She hadn't even called to say she'd be late.

Finally, she crawled into the front seat to find her coat. Where the heck were her shoes? She felt along the floor and found them. She held her breath, trying to drum up the courage to open the passenger side door. *It's now or never.*

Over the top of the car, she saw the group—five of them, including her supposed boyfriend. Two of the boys held flashlights aimed at the ground while they spoke in low voices. There was a girl she didn't recognize who nodded and smiled whenever the boys laughed, reminding her of Taylor. In the dark, she could have easily been Taylor's twin with her slim build and long dark hair.

The kids immediately stopped talking when they saw Hannah. She ignored them and stared at Deacon. He glanced at her then turned back to his conversation. Hannah felt the anger rising up both sides of her head, her jaw clenching until it hurt. She crossed her forearms and leaned them on top of the car. Soon her head followed, folding onto them. Her once-sweaty body began to shiver.

Hannah's mind raced between making a scene and obediently getting back in the car. She didn't like either option. Then two of the boys, including one with a flashlight, reached into their pockets, and one of them raised two fingers, leading Deacon to pull two bags from inside his trench coat. Hannah felt momentarily bewildered that he had drugs on him, and then realized her naiveté. *He's a dealer, not a Boy Scout.*

Deacon and Hannah barely said a word to one another driving back to her house, and even less when she slammed the car door behind her.

CHAPTER 21

"STAY AWAY FROM HER," TAYLOR'S MOM TOLD HER DAUGHTER when Hannah passed their house Friday morning to catch the bus. Hannah rolled her eyes and pressed on.

Taylor's mom reminded Hannah of one of those impossibly skinny-legged models out of a Ralph Lauren catalog, complete with her plaid headband (like mother like daughter), uniform pearls, and crewneck top, paired smartly with her never-been-on-a-horse equestrian pants and stylish heels. She exuded enough pep and false empathy to equal a gymnasium full of Garden Club groupies. Hannah imagined that those gratuitous hugs she'd seen her bestow on her lady friends in public were really barbed wire in disguise once backs were turned.

Taylor definitely favored her mother in the looks department. She was by far the real beauty between the two of them, but still, her mom looked pretty great for her age. Hannah wondered what it was like for Taylor to have a hot mom who strutted around like she owned the town, her spry, wiry body wrapping itself around all the right people.

It's fine, Hannah told herself, shrugging off Taylor's mom's words. Those girls didn't mean much to her now. It was actually a relief to not be so preoccupied with them and trying to fit into their fake world. The real problem now was with Deacon and the never-ending stream of losers who appeared out of nowhere wherever he went, like at school or in the park when they were making out last night.

Luckily, her parents had been upstairs when she got home and didn't seem to have noticed her absence. Kerry and her mom went to bed early, while her dad stared at the downstairs TV late into the evening. Still Hannah tortured herself, tossing in bed, running through everything that happened. Deacon hadn't called and she was sure he was pissed. Times like this, she didn't even know what they had together. Obviously not good communication skills. Was it *just* physical between them? But he didn't pressure her sexually and had moved pretty slowly so far, she reasoned, especially for a senior. He could be so sweet with her, too—protective, even.

But his ever-present beeper was definitely the third wheel in their relationship.

Hannah chewed on the ends of her hair, telling herself that what he did on the side didn't matter. She thought about what Peter said. Was Deacon putting her in danger? She knew she was falling for him and becoming more dependent on their relationship. She'd hated her life before him, and the thought of them being done summoned a lump in the back of her throat. She tucked the wet strands of hair behind her ear. *Did I just screw the whole thing up?*

"Hey," Hannah said, sliding into the seat next to Peter. The bus's screeching air brakes sounded louder than normal against Peter's silence. *It's just as well*, Hannah thought, feeling her stomach drop as the bus chugged up the final hill to school like the train in one of Kerry's favorite books, *The Little Engine That Could.*

She closed her eyes, thinking of what she was going to say to Deacon . . . if he was even waiting for her.

"Read the assignment for Myers's class?"

Hannah opened her eyes. The furthest thing from her mind was homework. "Yeah, it sucked. So boring."

"For sure," Peter said, giving her a small smile.

"Now you sound like a Valley Girl."

"Fer sure, fer sure. She's a Valley Girl," Peter sang, mimicking that infectious Frank and Moon Zappa song that still played unmercifully on the radio.

"Gag me with a spoon," she teased back, relieved that they'd moved past their awkward moment.

Hannah stepped off the bus, knowing that Deacon wouldn't be waiting for her. Taking a deep breath, she walked up the long path into school, dreading what awaited her behind its large steel-gray doors.

She soldiered on through the crowded hallway, rounding the bend toward homeroom, and that's when she saw the black trench coat and crossed combat boots leaning leisurely against her locker, watching her make her way through the stream of kids. She immediately felt something pick her up by the elbows and practically float her over to him, and she knew he could see it too. She tried not to smile, averting her eyes, but it was too late. He kissed her forehead and held his face close to hers. She inhaled his delicious, spicy scent, and tilted up her face to kiss him once then again, this time longer. His lips were warm and soft, inviting her back into his world. Her chest twisted with a longing to be alone with him, like they had been in the park. She pulled back, hoping to see her thoughts reflected in his eyes, but she couldn't read them. A white blur caught her eye: in his hand was a long-stemmed rose.

"Wow, didn't see that coming. It's beautiful," she said softly.

"For you ... for yesterday."

She pursed her lips, stripping them of color, then brought the flower to her nose, letting the creamy petal caress her upper lip. *Wait, this doesn't erase what happened*, the voice in her head wailed. *But this isn't the place*, she told it. Besides, how could she *now?* She managed a small smile and he drew her into his arms. She surrendered to his lips once again and it felt right—more than right, it fed her. Hannah floated back into her dream world where it was just the two of them, alone and always feeling like this. Dizzily, she opened her eyes to watch him kiss her. But instead, she caught him staring at something behind her. A dark shadow crept across his eyes before he pulled away.

"Let's go," he said with a sigh.

"Okay, one sec, let me get my books first." Hannah fumbled with her locker, aware that Deacon's body was shifting with impatience. She looked to either side of her. The hallway was empty.

Fucking white rose. Toby smirked. He pulled on his varsity football jacket and ran his fingers through his thick auburn hair, glancing around to see if anyone was checking him out.

No one was. His eyes rested again on the picture of the famous family he'd cut from the newspaper and taped to the back of his locker where you could only see it if you'd emptied the space of all its contents.

He glowered at them, the fairy-tale family—wholesomely promoted, never ostentatious, perfectly manicured and maintained like one of those lawn commercials. Toby guffawed, letting his spit fly in their faces: the esteemed, enviable parents, good-looking and capable in their own right, each with a hand on the shoulder of their ever-dashing, popular teenage son, all dressed in black.

CHAPTER 22

"HANNAH! GET THE HELL OUT HERE," HER FATHER CALLED, storming through the house. Hannah quickly pushed her math book aside and opened her bedroom door. An audible gasp escaped from her lips as she stepped nervously back into her room. Her father's face burned purple with rage. His yard jacket was covered in leaves, and clumps of mud traipsed along his sleeve—all the way down to the stepstool shaking in his hand.

Oh Christ, the stepstool!

"What the hell is *this?*" he spat.

"I-I don't know, Dad," Hannah stammered. *Think, think!* "Maybe Kerry was playing with it outside?"

"How do you know I found it outside?"

Shit. "The mud?"

"I fell over this in the flowerbed under your bedroom window. There were muddy shoe marks on the siding, Hannah!"

"Dad . . . I don't have any . . ."

"Have you been sneaking out? You . . . you *whore!*"

"No, I haven't. Dad, stop! *Please.*" Hannah tried to close her door, but his left arm shot out and blocked it as he took two more steps into her room, spraying the mud across her floor.

"Stop, Daddy! Stop!" Her bedroom began to swirl like a merry-go-round; she was falling, really falling. Her legs folded underneath her, and the carpet rose up toward her face. She caught herself before her nose hit. Slumping to the ground like a rag doll, she begged for it to stop: her dad's yells, the spinning room, for it all to stop.

Whore. Whore. Whore.

Hannah didn't know how long it was before she opened her eyes, but when she looked back at her doorway, he was gone.

She stumbled out of her room to the kitchen. Her hands fumbled with the phone. *Please, please be home*, she prayed.

He answered on the second ring.

"Deacon, I have to get out of here. Can you come get me?"

"You had a flashback from the trip. It happens." He sighed and stroked her hair until she felt like she was going to pass out. If she could just die in Deacon's arms right then, sitting in his car around the block from her house, Hannah thought, that would be all right by her.

"How can I ever go back?" she asked, setting off a fresh wave of tears. Her thumbs ached, and for a moment she thought about how much she loved to suck them as a child.

"Shhh, don't worry about that. It's all going to blow over. Eventually, he'll forget about it. They all do," he said, staring out the front window. It was beginning to rain.

"I can't go back there!" Hannah cried.

He pulled her into his arms. She felt broken and small.

"Where do you want to go, then?" he whispered into her hair.

"Anywhere but here."

Deacon's house was perched on top of the tallest hill in town, peering down at the rows of cookie-cutter homes below. The mansion, replicated from an old English Tudor in South Wales, bore a brass plaque at its driveway entrance with the name Highfield Manor inscribed in it. Hannah couldn't recall visiting a home with a name before—except for her fifth grade field trip to the White House, but that didn't really count.

The mansions to either side measured equally in size and beauty, but the Giroux abode exuded an edge of glamour, as if an exotic sheik and not a mere politician lived there. Its twisting driveway wound visitors up the massive grounds, enclosing them in scrolls of wrought iron fencing with sharp spear points and coiling vines.

Hannah tried to act cool, but she couldn't help herself. "Dude, you live *here*?" she said in disbelief. "It's huge! If this were my house, I'd never leave. You're like that rich guy in that *Arthur* movie."

"Don't be so sure," Deacon replied coolly, his clenched jaw sending the hollows of his cheeks inward. His sleek countenance seemed on the verge of fracturing, but he quickly flashed his candy cane smile at her, and his control was back.

They walked up the wide cobblestone path to the towering double doors, which were flanked by a pair of greyhound statues, both pooches looking ready to pounce. Above them, menacing brass lion doorknockers roared their disdain.

Deacon slipped his arm around her waist and gripped her firmly. She wondered which one of them he was protecting. To Hannah, they were entering a rich person's wild kingdom, carefully guarded and yet charged with an imposing air of importance. She felt lightheaded with anticipation; maybe she'd see a bearskin rug or something inside.

They stood there at the massive doors, letting the drizzle hit their faces. Confused, Hannah looked up at Deacon.

"Yeah, I don't have a key," he said weirdly, then wheeled her around toward the garage.

"Ah, why?"

"Parents." He shrugged. "Front door is just for show. We don't actually use it."

"Lots of animals."

"That's my mom. Wait until you see inside," he said as he entered the garage code.

Hannah thought she had just walked into a classic car showroom when she stepped into the Girouxs' garage. She counted four—no, five—shiny vintage sports cars in a row, each one a more eye-popping candy color than the next. The space screamed cleanliness and was meticulously organized. Hannah thought one could eat off its checkered black-and-white floor tiles—a far cry from the Zandana family's dank single-car garage stuffed with junk.

Deacon immediately removed his boots, and Hannah followed suit. "My mom's a neat freak," he said, shaking his head, his eyes avoiding hers.

"Listen, if this is a bad idea—"

"No, it's fine," he replied, cutting her off. Taking her hand, he walked her through a long, dark hallway, which opened up to a two-story circular foyer that resembled a cage. Hannah looked up, imagining raw meat being thrown down to its captives. Dark wood moldings secured its walls to the ornamented ceiling, while a huge pedestal table with lion claw feet commanded center stage on top of a blood-red oriental rug.

She immediately noticed the oversized oil painting of a lioness on the opposing wall, depicted after a kill, apparently: her prey was under one foot and there were traces of blood around her throat. *Creepy*, Hannah thought, and she absently touched the front of her neck and wrapped her other arm around herself. Her eyes widened as she absorbed the scope of the room, but Deacon seemed unaffected and aloof; he swiftly moved her into the next two rooms.

The living room was a continuation of the menagerie, with several mounted animal heads sporting jagged antlers on the walls, their terrified glass eyes screaming *Leave now.*

"This is where Babette . . . hangs," Deacon said, motioning toward the parlor room just adjacent. His mom's space felt lighter compared to the rest of the house, a break from the wildness. It contained a mix of pastels and chintz fabrics—expertly thrown together by the hand of a decorator, no doubt. Curious, Hannah picked up one of the books from the glass coffee table. Deacon's mom read the romances, just like her mom.

"And here's old man Kingsley's . . ."

"Study," said Hannah, finishing his sentence. As predicted, there sprawled in the center of the paneled room, surrounded by two tufted leather couches and a heavy wooden desk, lay the final resting place of a massive white bear with its mouth agape—razor-like teeth revealed and gleaming.

Hannah jumped. "You could have warned me," she chided.

"Where's the fun in that?" he teased, coming up behind her and grabbing her shoulders. Hannah's attention was already preoccupied with trying to read the book titles on the massive shelves when he started to kiss her neck—at first gently, then more ardently. He turned her toward him, finding her lips. And at first she was enjoying it—but then, suddenly, he trapped her head and body in a vise grip, leaving her with no chance for air or escape.

She had become the prey.

Hannah pushed back at him, searching his face. "Wait, wait . . . are we alone?"

"Yeah." As soon his response left his lips, he expertly reclined her on the nearest leather couch. He seemed possessed, kissing her body and pulling her blouse from her jeans. Hannah's eyes darted to either side of the room, trying to think of something to slow him down, worried that she'd somehow brought this on by suggesting they come here.

She lifted up his head. "Deacon, wait! We shouldn't be in here, in your dad's study. What if they come home?"

He continued to kiss her, unbuttoning her blouse and grinding himself into her more fervently. Hannah tried to roll him off of her, but his determination only grew stronger, from his mouth down to his desire, which was now protruding from his jeans. For the first time, Hannah felt afraid.

A car door slammed outside, and Hannah, with all her might, pushed him off of her. "Deacon, your parents!"

They scrambled to his mother's parlor, frantically tucking in shirts and smoothing down hair—mostly Hannah's—and fell onto one of the chintz settees. They both caught their breath and attempted to appear nonchalant, but Hannah knew their flushed faces and the electricity still radiating between their bodies were going to give them away. She held a peach pastel pillow against her chest and twirled a section of her hair as she awaited her first meeting with Deacon's esteemed parental units.

Deacon shifted in his seat at the sound of the garage door opening, followed by the thunder of high heels echoing through the hallway like a galloping horse. *How fitting*, Hannah thought. Then someone began coughing—a male clearing the mucus encrusting his throat—and they heard car keys carelessly sliding across the expensive wooden foyer table. In response, the high heels marched louder.

"There you are," Deacon's mother said, hesitating in the doorway. Classical music began almost on cue in another part of the house as Babette Giroux sauntered into the room, smoother than a runway model in her quilted Chanel suit, dripping in long strands of black and white embellished pearls. Hannah immediately caught the disapproval in her skinny lips, which were holding a line like a tightrope.

"Well, isn't this cozy?"

"Hi, Mrs. Giroux, I'm Hannah." She extended her hand, unsure if she should stand or not.

"Pleasure," Babette said icily, her floral perfume snuffing out the oxygen in the room. She ignored Hannah's hand and snatched the peach pillow from her lap, replacing it with an old-looking maroon one she'd surreptitiously pulled from somewhere. "Oil from the hands stains," she said, coiling one of her pearl strands around her fingers. She appeared transfixed by Hannah's erupting skin and the growing blotches crawling across her neck and chest. Babette's lips moved soundlessly, like she was counting something. Hannah clenched the curls in her hand harder.

Babette's bosom swelled once, and then she slowly turned and slithered out of the room.

Hannah couldn't take her eyes off Deacon's mom until she'd disappeared from sight. It seemed Babette carried her curves in all the right places, from her ample, fleshy chest to her upside-down heart-shaped bottom. Her creamy calves held their own like supple raw chicken breasts.

Hannah turned to Deacon, trying to read his face.

"Now you know," he said, staring straight ahead, looking sadder than Hannah had ever seen him.

She took his hand in hers and kissed it. "Let's go."

Hannah's mind filled up with questions she desperately wanted answered during the ride back to her house. The car's digital clock read 6:34 p.m. *Shoot, later than I thought.*

"Deacon—"

"I'm ditching school Monday, so I can't give you a ride home."

"Where are you going?" Hannah asked, surprised that he hadn't mentioned it before.

"I've got to meet some people in the city. Work stuff." Hannah imagined that he had to stock up on drugs and his supplier must be in New York City. Then something dawned on her.

"Who are you going with?"

Deacon hesitated and glanced out his back window. "You don't know them," he said, trying for nonchalance but failing.

"Try me," Hannah pressed.

"Jade and Bobby, couple of the kids from the other night." Who the hell was Jade? Hannah's mind raced, running through the girls in her class, but couldn't place anyone with that unusual name. She didn't know many juniors or seniors.

They stopped at a light across from Gossamer Park. Deacon began singing "Sunglasses at Night," tapping the steering wheel to the music. Hannah gazed out her window, still wondering about the girl, when she spotted a huge oak tree on the corner of the park's entrance. *The girl standing with the boys in the park*—that's who he was talking about. Hannah's anxiety traveled down her arms and into her hands. She resisted the urge to drill him further.

"Hey, it's no big deal. I go all the time," he said, squeezing her thigh before turning up the block to her house. Hannah didn't want to start a fight and wasn't sure what she was feeling. Her Sunday afternoon had been all too surreal, starting with her father yelling about the stepstool and the scary LSD flashback, then being in Deacon's house for the first time and him practically attacking her in his father's study—and all of that capped off by his mother accusing her of having greasy hands.

"Okay, see you when you get back," she said, delivering her best chilled-out voice.

"You going to kiss me or what?" Deacon said, sounding angry—but the corners of his mouth turned up, giving him away.

"Or what?" she teased back, leaning in to give him a

quick peck. He grabbed her face and pulled her in for a longer kiss. Hannah let out a tight laugh and backed herself out of the car.

Before going inside, she stood and watched him fly back up the street. She didn't feel like going inside; the November night air felt good against her skin. She closed her eyes, taking a needed moment to clear her head before facing her parents. A chill ran through her shoulders when she thought about Deacon and how he'd acted like a different person at his house and even cagier on the ride home, like something had set him off. His dark, romantic way scared her as much as it seduced her, she thought, bringing her fingertips to her lips. There also lay an undeniable beauty in his melancholy. One that she longed to heal.

Hannah glanced back at her house. She shook her head and walked up the driveway, comparing Deacon's insanely sprawling abode to her barely inhabitable squalor. Tonight it seemed even more unwelcoming, with every light off, the garage strangely open, and her parents' paneled station wagon gone. *Weird.*

"Mom? Dad?" Hannah tentatively called when she got inside.

Nothing. No signs of life.

She flipped on the kitchen light, then circled back into the living room and flopped on the couch. She wondered how she was going to face her father when he got home and how long he'd ground her for this time.

The phone rang, interrupting her thoughts. *It has to be them*, she thought—then worried that they had called the house more than once looking for her.

"Hello?"

"Listen, the way my mom treated you, it's just messed up."

"Thanks for saying—" Hannah stopped when she heard the sound of a car horn, followed by more street noises. "Hey, where are you?"

"Outside Gossamer Park. At the payphone."

"Deacon, it's getting late. Are you sure that's such a good idea?"

"Just one more transaction, then I'm out of here."

She took a breath. "I don't know what's going on with us. You were so strange in your dad's study, in the car. I wish we could—"

"Yep, that's them. Gotta go."

Hannah held the receiver in her hand, letting the dial tone numb her ear. Warm tears stung her eyes as she stood in her hollow kitchen, surrounded by grime and neglect, watching the starburst clock clip away the seconds of her sad, pathetic life.

CHAPTER 23

HANNAH PAUSED HALFWAY THROUGH HER BOWL OF CEREAL and found her father standing in front of her, his broad body turned to the side, forcing her to read his profile.

"Your sister swallowed one of your mother's medications. They pumped her stomach. She's at County. Your mom's with her," he said, stiff as a soldier.

Water droplets rolled down his matted hair and coat onto the floor, creating small pools around his feet. He stared at the car keys he'd just slid across the counter and frowned.

Hannah's response lodged in her throat, making her spew her milk across the table when she tried to force it out. She quickly wiped it up with her sleeve, then pulled the sleeve over her hand and clenched the wetness underneath the table.

"I'm going to bed," her father said, studying the same kitchen cabinet for several seconds, burning a hole in its contents: little yellow and blue pills nestled behind the wine glasses. His arms stuck frozen at his sides.

"How . . ."

"And you're grounded," he added, turning away and leaving with his usual piece of her.

That's it? How the hell did this happen? Hannah screamed inside as her lips began to twitch, her shoulders now trembling. She wrapped her arms around them, longing to be held, still nodding even after he'd walked away. *Oh Kerry, oh little Kerry.* She wished she could head over to County now to see her, but she didn't dare ask. Her father's face looked ravaged and chewed up; his anger was still bubbling.

The doorbell rang, making her jump.

"I'll get it," she called, running to the foyer, hoping it was Deacon. Maybe he could give her a ride to the hospital.

She yanked open the door, but it was just that jock, Toby.

"Deacon around?" he said, trying to push past her for a look into her house. She could feel her dad behind her, standing in the hallway, and knew that she didn't have much time.

"No," she said firmly, putting a hand up to his chest.

"Do you know where he is?" he persisted, taking a couple steps back, self-consciously running his fingers through his hair. It was then that Hannah noticed the babyishness of his chipmunk-cheek face, a sharp contrast to his muscular manbody. He wasn't as tall as Deacon, but he carried his wide shoulders stiffly, his curved Popeye arms making him look like a bodybuilder on steroids. He grinned every other second—a nervous tic, it seemed—and had deep dimples that created quotation marks around his mouth and chin. His wide brown eyes and the smattering of freckles across his nose only magnified his gullible appearance.

There was something familiar in his dark eyes, too—something she couldn't place. He was somewhat cute in a puffed-up Michelin Man sort of way, but his jittery manner annoyed Hannah.

"He's in Gossamer Park, I think." Hannah wished she had stopped talking as soon as the words left her mouth;

Deacon didn't need this guy following him around trying to cop some drugs.

"He's not answering his beeper."

"I have no idea," she said, shaking her head, getting irritated.

"It's cool," he said, shrugging and looking away.

She closed the door. Her dad was frozen in the same stance, one hand on the railing, gazing down at his feet like he wanted to tell her something. She waited, bracing herself. But no words came. She watched him slowly ascend the long flight of stairs.

Monday morning on the bus, Hannah tried to look attentive as Peter rambled on about some show he'd watched the night before—*Tales from the Crypt* or something. He was definitely getting more comfortable around her. Hannah tried to smile and nod in appropriate places, but she really wasn't following his critique. She had tossed and turned most of the night thinking about her sister and what could have possibly happened to make her swallow her mother's pills, especially when Flintstone Chewable Vitamins were usually a chore to get down her. When she wasn't mulling over that, she was thinking about Deacon and where things were going with them. She awoke exhausted.

The drone of Peter's voice was a welcome distraction from the noise in her head. She knew school would drag on forever with Deacon out today, but there was still hope that they'd see each other tomorrow, Election Day, since they had it off from school. She was sure they could figure something out, even though she was grounded.

Suddenly, Peter stopped talking and stared at her.

"Sorry, I missed that—still waking up, I guess," Hannah said. "What?"

"Do you want to see a movie tomorrow?"

"I'm grounded," she said, slinging her book bag over her shoulder. *Oh my gosh, did he just ask me out? Weird.*

She was saved by their arrival at school. "Well, see you later!" she said, hastily, and made her escape.

"Yo, Z!"

Toby was waiting for her near the bottom of the bus's steps, his bellowing voice causing every head nearby to turn.

She decided to play it cool. "So, did you ever find him last night?" she asked as Toby began walking with her into school. *Okay, this is even weirder.*

"Ah, no," he said, looking annoyed. "No, the asshole didn't show. We were supposed to meet today. Where is he?"

"The city."

"Shit, really?"

Hannah glanced around self-consciously. His jumpy manner was drawing people's attention.

"So, how long have you guys been going out?"

"Over a month, I guess."

"Seems longer." Toby drifted away from her and stopped in front of Gillian and Taylor, who were talking at their lockers. She realized then that the two of them must have gotten a ride that morning.

"Hey you!" purred Taylor in her gooey-sweet, singsong voice.

Oh great, now they're all friends, Hannah thought and picked up the pace

CHAPTER 24

DEACON FELT LIKE A KID AMONG THE SWARM OF commuters buzzing around him when he stepped off the train at Grand Central Station. No one took particular notice of him, it seemed. Many of them, especially the few females he saw, appeared to be late for wherever they were headed and stressed out. He watched them take flight into the grand concourse. He couldn't imagine his mother running in the same circle as these workingwomen, each of them out to prove something—"He-women," as Babette liked to call them.

He quickly moved aside to let one of them—a woman carrying an expensive-looking briefcase and wearing a long, double-breasted coat with leather lapels and her commuter sneakers—zip in front of him. He was in no rush for what he had to do today. He hung back instead with the men, who walked noticeably slower in their shiny wingtips, wool topcoats, and fat gold watches, each of them dripping with more success than the last.

Jade and Bobby were taking a later train, giving him just enough time to make the call he'd been dreading since he woke up. *Let's get this deal over with.*

The first two payphones he found had severed receiver

cords, making him feel like a jackass since he'd already put a quarter in each of them before realizing it. The third one was in a more remote part of the terminal—not ideal, but at least it worked.

"Yo."

"Tell him I'm coming by in a few . . . I don't know, twenty to twenty-five rocks or so . . . yes, cash," Deacon said. He hung up the grimy receiver, which smelled like a nasty buffet of puke and malt liquor—and just then, a creepy feeling came over him. He turned to find a guy waiting behind him for the phone wearing a ripped NEW YORK, NEW YORK! sweatshirt and carrying a filthy pillowcase filled with God knew what. The stranger was standing far too close for Deacon's liking.

They locked eyes. The older man's straggly, unwashed hair and sunken, strung-out face prompted Deacon to move out of the way, but he held the stranger's stare. He dug his hands into his coat pockets with feigned resolve and turned to walk out onto East 42nd Street; he looked back once, but the guy had disappeared, the phone receiver dangling helplessly over the ground. *Better make this quick*, he told himself.

He walked as fast as he could to his destination, pushed the button to call up, and waited. He could barely hear the electronic door's speaker over the noise from the street, and it seemed to take forever to get buzzed in, which only added to the nerves racing inside of him. He scanned both sides of the sidewalk for cops before walking through the double-glass doors into the vestibule. The stench from the narrow, ill-lit hallway overwhelmed him—human body odor mixed with fecal waste, reminding him of a train station bathroom but a million times magnified.

His eyes slowly adjusted, and he spotted the shapes of three people down at the far end. He started to lose his nerve and thought about turning around, but by now they'd seen him. He cursed himself for bringing so much cash. Then he heard the sound of a lighter and caught a halo of light moving in small circles under a pipe, warming and liquefying its contents into pure gold, illuminating three eager faces. One belonged to a woman with the longest, skinniest arms and legs Deacon had ever seen, followed tragically by her expectant belly. He suddenly felt sick.

The sound of the popping got louder as he passed the three gaunt junkies intent on getting their high. He knew the transaction would be swift once he was inside, but still his heart pummeled inside his chest. He thought of Hannah and wished he were home with her. He counted two more doors and knocked softly.

A tall, lanky kid, the one who'd probably spoken with him on the phone, opened the door slowly. He was dressed like he'd just come off a rap video, decked in parachute pants with a matching track jacket. The small room smelled of Vanillaroma car freshener, and held little furniture except for two white armchairs flanking a square, black-lacquered table. Most of the supplier's stash was hidden elsewhere, Deacon presumed, for very little was laid out in front of him.

He presented his cash with little preamble, noticing the soiled mattress in the corner on the floor—probably for those who needed to "pay" another way—as he handed over the bills.

The skinny kid performed most of the transaction; the other guy—a heavy, older man—just sat solemnly, clasping his pudgy hands over his voluminous belly. He wore a flourish of gilded medallions, as if he was an Olympian. Deacon felt the older man's eyes sizing him up, and he didn't like it; as soon as the kid handed him the drugs, he grabbed them, nodded, and quickly got out of there.

Deacon stepped around the extended legs of the three junkies in the hallway, holding his trench coat around his legs to avoid brushing against them, as he exited. Their vacant eyes stared off eerily, their brief fix dangerously deflating.

He caught the blue-uniformed cop out of the corner of his eye, not more than a few yards away, right as he swung open the exterior glass doors. With his stomach in his throat, the bag of rocks bulging inside his coat, and his legs forgetting how to walk, he forced himself to keep moving, seeing his father's face the whole time.

Bobby was kissing Jade near one of the broken payphones in the terminal, his hands roaming up and down her back, when Deacon walked past them. He cleared his throat, and Bobby broke their embrace. The two of them inconspicuously fell in line several feet behind him. Suburban teens ditching school for a day in the city: that was the plan Deacon had told them. So they'd dressed and were acting the part. The tall lacrosse player wore his country-club good looks well in a preppy pink Lacoste shirt and pink sweater, his blond hair carefully combed to the side; and Jade, green-eyed and olive-skinned, had donned tight designer jeans and a matching denim jacket adorned with a handful of concert pins across her chest. Her long, dark, china doll hair swayed as she strutted hand in hand with Bobby, clearly enjoying the eyes that followed her. Together, they made an ideal distraction.

Deacon shook his head at the charade, especially Jade's, questioning her taste in lovers—first Gillian, now Bobby. He'd never seen much in her himself, but she'd been the first one in the park that night to volunteer for the city run, which had surprised him.

Dealing the rock would take his business to a whole other level. It hooked customers hard on their very first try, it was cheap to get, and it provided an intense, fifteen-minute high. Just to get another hit, Deacon knew his fellow (rich) classmates would steal off their parents, friends, even their little sisters' piggybanks. His mouth watered just thinking about the amount of cash he could easily pull in—up to a few thousand a day. He could almost taste the power.

His growing reputation for having the "good stuff" had unfortunately made him a walking target. Increasingly, the wrong types of people were finding out that he carried both drugs and plenty of cash. For that reason, Deacon never stashed his drugs in his car or at home anymore; he placed them in crumbling walls around school and occasionally at acquaintances' houses without them knowing, to keep them secure. That weekend of Hannah's LSD trip, he had even stored some in her bedroom. Which reminded him: they were due for another nighttime rendezvous.

CHAPTER 25

"KERRY, ARE YOU OKAY?"

Her sister's boney back protruded from her denim coveralls, and her scalloped pink turtleneck made her appear smaller and more fragile than the last time Hannah had seen her. She entered the little bedroom—once her own childhood nursery, decorated in blues and yellows, but now exploding in Pepto-Bismol pink, from the walls down to the ruffled curtains and matching bedspread. Kerry's dainty dresser and shelves corralled a barnyard of stuffed animals in every color and size. She was crazy about animals: horses, sheep, even frogs, it didn't matter. Their father seemed to buy her a new stuffed something every other week.

Kerry was currently playing with her beloved Droge bear, the one she slept with every night. His name came from Kerry's mispronunciation of "droopy drawers," the moniker her parents gave her when she first started walking because of the way her diaper hung between her pudgy legs. Hannah smiled at the memory as she watched Kerry stroke her beloved bear's matted, thoroughly sucked-on fur with a sense of purpose. Her sister's little lips were pressed into a pout, her little legs dangling motionless off the bed.

"Kerry?"

Her sister stopped petting her bear for a moment. Then the sound of a boy riding his bike and calling to someone down the street pulled her attention toward her window, and she gazed out through the glass, ignoring her sister.

Hannah waited. She couldn't remember the last time Kerry had had a friend over. She seemed to spend all of her time either obsessively monopolizing their mother's attention or getting engrossed in another episode of *Little House on the Prairie.*

Hannah walked slowly around the bed, searching Kerry's face for any possible clue to what had happened and why, but stopped short, horrified, when she saw the dark, purplish circles under her baby sister's eyes.

"Kerry, can you tell me what happened?" Her voice caught. She wanted to put her arm around her little sister and rub her back—to somehow make the scary accident and ordeal in the hospital all go away. "Was it because of *me?*" she asked in a small voice, afraid to know the answer. "Maybe because you saw me take a couple pills when I broke my nose, so I could sleep?"

She felt guilty and cursed herself for not spending more time with her little sister. All Hannah had ever wanted as a little girl was to have a big sister—someone to share stuff with and show her how to deal with the kids at school. Now *she* was that big sister, and apparently a pretty crappy one.

Kerry stared silently at the bear cradled in her lap. After a moment, her tiny voice came out in a whisper. "I wanted . . . to be like Mommy. I pretended, by taking her golden pills. They always made her so happy. I wanted to feel happy, like Mommy."

Hannah closed her eyes, seeing her mother asleep in her car outside and the way she staggered back into the house. *No, no, no!*

"I started taking tranquilizers to calm my nerves," her mom said, suddenly appearing like a ghost in the doorframe, her voice casual and nonchalant, as if everyone in town medicated themselves whenever the mood struck.

What "nerves" exactly? Hannah wondered. Her mom wouldn't meet her questioning face; instead, she poured her attention into her youngest daughter like she was a box of Cracker Jacks, her glassy pupils eyeing the prize inside.

"Kerry thought they were candy, that's all. Right, honey?"

Hannah wanted to scream at her mother and the game she was playing. *Is that what you told the hospital, Mom?* Then she saw Kerry's tiny elbow jerk back, ripping off pieces of fur from her Droge bear, her teeth clenched, her eyes fierce with resolve. They both watched Kerry attack her beloved bear and take it apart bit by bit, rolling each clump of fur between her thumb and middle finger into a tight little ball before placing it inside one nostril, then the other, alternating sides while she worked.

Hannah felt the heat rise in her neck. She sucked at the air that was trying to escape from her lungs. Like a deranged dollhouse come to life, the tiny, pink, ruffled bedroom started closing in on them. The upper walls tilted inward, forming a tent that began scraping the little bedroom's white, immaculate ceiling, making Hannah duck for cover.

The black marble eyes of Kerry's stuffed animals suddenly spun and grew in size as the whole barnyard pulsated off the dresser and shelves. Neither Kerry nor their mom took notice. Not wanting to share her hallucination, Hannah kept silent. She kept closing and opening her eyes, madly trying to decipher what was real and what wasn't. *This is all in my imagination. None of this is happening.* But then, like a dance Hannah had seen too many times before, her mother began stroking her youngest daughter's hair, humming an unrecognizable tune as Kerry fleeced her favorite, most trusted bear, lodging more and more fur balls up her nose. Hannah had to look away, feeling sick. When she did, the walls and the stuffed animals gradually stopped their show. But the reality of what was left terrified her most of all.

CHAPTER 26

"HELLO?" SHE WHISPERED. HER THROAT FELT LIKE SAND-
paper, her voice rough. She'd pulled the phone into her room
after her parents had gone to bed.

"Hi."

"What time is it?"

"After ten."

"I must have dozed off . . . waiting."

"Sorry."

"So, how was your trip into the city?"

"Fine, I guess. Jade pissed me off. Long story."

"Try me."

Deacon exhaled into the phone. "We almost got busted
coming back on the train. An undercover cop asked Bobby
some questions and Jade started to freak out. Nearly blew it.
The guy's been following me around with his partner. I didn't
see him until it was too late."

"Kerry overdosed on my mother's Valium."

"Shit."

"Happened yesterday, when I was at your house . . . they
pumped her stomach and everything."

"Geez, she okay?"

"I'm not sure," Hannah said, feeling the back of her throat contract. "I had another flashback, this time in front of my mom and sister . . . a bad one."

"Oh my god, that sucks . . . I'm really sorry, Hannah. I wish I'd never given it to you. I kick myself just thinking about it."

She could hear the tenderness in his voice and wished she could see his face—see his chocolate brown eyes and red pouty lips making it all better.

"About tomorrow . . . I was thinking, let's hang out, just us."

"I'd like that," she said, trying to conceal the excitement in her voice. She couldn't stop smiling and knew she probably looked ridiculous; she was glad he couldn't see her face. One call from him and everything was suddenly right in the world.

"Pick you up, then?"

Hannah's mind raced. How would she get out of the house without her parents noticing? But she couldn't miss this chance to have some alone time with Deacon. She would figure it out.

"Most definitely."

———

She felt quite glamorous strolling up the grand staircase with Deacon that morning. They exchanged knowing looks and shared a playful giddiness over the fact that they had the house to themselves while Deacon's parents were out conducting their last-minute campaign rounds. Hannah was supposedly at the library, studying all day for exams. It hadn't been too hard to convince her parents to let her go, especially with them being so preoccupied with Kerry. Her mother just seemed relieved that Hannah had someplace to go.

She ran her fingertips along the dark oak banister, taking in the opulent décor for a second time, fantasizing for a moment that she and Deacon were married and this was their house, where every night he'd take her up to the bedroom and have his way with her. Hannah chuckled at the thought.

"What?"

"Oh, nothing," she said, grinning, feeling her cheeks flush.

Deacon closed the massive bedroom door behind him and on cue, Hannah's palms started to perspire. She turned and lowered her head to casually smell her armpit, but Deacon caught her and laughed.

"Wait, are we in your parents' bedroom?"

"No, mine."

It was nothing like she imagined. It looked more like a guest room than a bedroom for a teenage boy; it was decorated in dark paneling and sparse, antique-looking pieces, from the queen-size sleigh bed in the center of the room to the heavy, ornate matching bedside tables and floor-to-ceiling bookcases, all filled with leather-bound editions that appeared more for show than reading pleasure. It was void of boyhood knickknacks or any stuff at all, for that matter; in fact, the room contained little evidence of him actually living there. On the walls hung a couple of large oil paintings; both portraits of bearded men in decorated military uniforms that Hannah assumed were distant relatives.

"Your room . . . it's so grown-up."

"It's been the same ever since I moved back."

"Moved back?"

"Yeah, my mom had me live with my grandfather until I was fourteen."

"Really? Why?"

Deacon shrugged. "So, beautiful, how is that lovely schnoz of yours?" he teased, pulling her closer, his hands resting on her shoulders.

"Pretty much healed," she replied, scrunching up her nose and making him laugh.

"I'm really glad you're here," he said, turning serious, his hands running underneath her hair and cupping the back of her neck. Hannah shivered at his touch, aware again that she would be unable to move away from his grip if she wanted to. Something behind his eyes lured her in closer, though: the same unguarded look she'd seen when they were alone in the park talking. Gone were his candy cane smile and cavalier seductiveness. To Hannah, this felt real. It felt like love.

"What do you want to listen to?" he asked, walking over to the stereo—the only thing in the room that seemed like his.

"Anything."

Deacon pressed play without changing the cassette. "I just got this and can't stop listening to it."

Hannah recognized it immediately: "A Sort of Homecoming," off U2's new album, filled the air around them. Deacon draped his arms around her again, this time straddling his legs wide on either side of her, making it so the two of them were at eye level with one another. His hands found her hair again, gently grabbing fistfuls. Hannah closed her eyes, wanting his lips to find hers, realizing that he was the one she'd been hungry for her whole life.

"Deacon, I . . ."

"I'm going to take very good care of you," he said, and then he kissed her, tenderly. Hannah parted her lips and he met her tongue, pressing his body against her. With a stroke of his lips, he colored her cheeks, eyelids, and forehead like a painter, bringing every part of her face to life. Deacon moaned softly and moved lower, lightly sucking her neck as if it was the sweetest of nectars. "God, you smell so good," he said.

Hannah smiled. Apparently he hadn't a clue what *his* cologne did to her. His mouth found its way down to her collarbone, and suddenly his fingers started unbuttoning her blouse. Her whole being began to spin like a carousel, but not in a dizzying way—more like the part of the ride where everything starts to slow down and become clearer. She placed her hands over his chest to steady herself, and the ride came to a stop.

Deacon pulled her partially opened blouse over her head, exposing the sexiest bra she owned, a black satin one. It wasn't much, but it was far better than the array of white-pilled ones she'd scrounged through until she found this one in the back of her drawer.

"Mmm, that's coming off fast," he said approvingly, his eyes absorbing every inch of her, turning her cheeks crimson. She knew he'd probably just kissed off all of her makeup and tried not to obsess about it. She started to tuck her head into his chest but he held her back, spreading her arms wide.

"Look at me."

"I can't," she said, avoiding his stare. "I'm not used to someone looking at me the way you do."

Deacon lifted up her face with both hands like it was a chalice. "You're beautiful, Hannah."

His seriousness made her giggle, and she felt herself relax a bit.

He scooped her up in his arms and laid her across his bed, touching her head down last. Hannah pulled her hair away from her hot neck, and his pillows and comforter cooled her body. His bed was huge compared to hers; firm, too, and undeniably masculine with its dark, heavy wood and monochromatic, stone-gray bedding that looked pristinely pressed. *Geez*, Hannah thought, *it's like a fancy hotel*. The curved footboard momentarily gave her the feeling she was flying on a magic carpet. As long as she ignored the strange bearded men eyeing her from either wall with accusatory looks, Hannah felt sexy just lying in his bed.

"Now I want to see *you*," she commanded, propping herself on her elbows.

With a wicked smile, Deacon pulled his T-shirt over his head, revealing his impossibly toned abdomen and sculpted shoulders. He looked like a Calvin Klein model in his dark jeans. *Probably from those years of swimming*, Hannah thought. Their eyes never left one another as Deacon hovered over her, his hands resting on the bed on either side of her, one of his feet still on the floor.

"Wish I knew what you were thinking," she said, her fingertips tracing a heart on his smooth chest and summoning small goose bumps across his skin.

"Isn't it obvious?"

"What?"

"How I feel about you?"

"Not always."

Deacon's face dropped, and Hannah wished she hadn't said anything. He shrugged and looked back over his shoulder. Then, all at once, he turned his gaze back on her and stared right through her. "I wouldn't have invited you here if I didn't want to be with you."

"I know that," she said carefully, hiding the small panic rising in her chest. "But how do you *feel* . . . about me?"

Deacon shook his head "no" several times. The words seemed lodged in his throat. He swallowed hard. In a low voice, he finally uttered, "Nothing . . ." He cleared his throat. "Like nothing I ever felt before."

Hannah grinned. Without words, their bodies began moving together, and the rest of the world fell away.

CHAPTER 27

⸺

THE AFTERNOON SUN SLANTED THROUGH THE BEDROOM window, catching Hannah's eye. Her lashes fluttered open with a start, and she squinted around the room, trying to figure out where she was. After a few beats, she relaxed into the cocoon of Deacon's body, his pulse strumming her back, his shallow breathing tickling her ear. A brown, muscular arm and a heavy leg were wrapped tight around her, preventing her escape.

Hannah wanted to encapsulate the moment forever. No worries, no parents, and above all—no beeper. Just them. She and Deacon had been like two kids exploring one another's bodies, and it had felt amazingly freeing to put her insecurities aside and let herself go.

She stretched slightly, feeling deliriously alive, each of her senses sharpened and crisp, her body whole and exquisitely ripe. Deacon had transformed her world into a prism of color and possibility—a place where everything was in focus.

She watched him sleep, looking more peaceful than she'd ever seen. She studied every curve of his cinnamon complexion, his thick, feathery lashes and cherry lips, engraving it in her mind . . . in case it all was to disappear.

⸺

Deacon stirred, his body so heavy it was like he'd become one with the bed. For the first time in a long time, he'd slept hard—and blissfully uninterrupted. He pulled Hannah closer, wanting her to move her attention away from the window and onto him. He kissed her shoulder, and its delicate whiteness squirmed underneath him. She turned her smiling face to his, and he kissed her.

They didn't have much time. Soon he'd have to turn on his beeper, let it light up with crazed clients who would be crawling the walls by now. He didn't want to think about it, or about his parents coming home, silently shedding their coats, pouring themselves drinks, and heading to separate parts of the house without so much as a hello.

He didn't want to let her go. Not this one. Just the thought of Hannah leaving unsettled him. He didn't understand the pull he felt to her.

Deacon watched her shyly tie up her hair and drape his sheet around herself. She leaned over, grabbed the two Trojan wrappers from the floor, and crumpled them up in her hand before giving him a sly look and heading to the bathroom. He got a kick out of her combination of nervousness and unexpected bravado. She had been an indulgence for him right from the beginning, since the first time she poked him in the back to get his attention at school, like he was being struck by Cupid's arrow. He liked her sharp wit and the way her pretty eyes danced whenever she laughed. She was the knot inside his chest. In his bed alone with her, he had kissed her to tell her all the things he couldn't say. For now, that seemed to be enough.

Hannah returned ready to find the same boy she'd left in bed, but he was gone. Deacon's overcast eyes told a deeper story, one she couldn't read.

"What is it?"

Deacon rolled onto his side, and when she sat down on the edge of the bed still wearing his sheet, he slid an arm around her waist. She had cleaned up the best she could without taking a shower, but now a chill trickled down her back, causing her body to shudder. She touched his cheek tentatively, hoping her touch would encourage him to spill whatever it was that was bothering him.

"So the weekend of your 'trip' . . . what I saw . . ." Deacon swallowed hard, his eyes avoiding hers. "I don't know how to ask this . . . the way you were screaming . . . what did your dad do to you?"

Hannah's head swirled, and the color rose in her face, making her lightheaded and unable to mask the shame she suddenly felt.

"You never told me you saw that."

"I didn't want to upset you," he said, lightly strumming her hand.

"What did *you* think?"

"Did he *rape* you?"

Hannah flinched. Her gaze went to the paintings across the room. The two bearded men on the wall stared her down, demanding an answer. She felt little pricks rise across her back. She dug her nails into her shoulders and looked around for her clothes. The dark room felt cold and threatening now, the men seemed to be smirking at her. She wasn't safe and had to get out. She eyed the bathroom door, plotting her escape, but Deacon pulled on her hand, forcing her to look at him.

"It's okay," he said softly, sitting up to hold her.

"No," she whispered, shaking her head without looking at him.

"It's okay, I've told you how much my parents suck—"

"I mean no, he didn't . . . my dad has a terrible temper. Always has. He can be fine one moment, but the next he's on top of you." Hannah stopped, realizing the tremendous irony of her words, and tried to find a way to explain. "He's crazy religious in a 'hell and damnation' kind of way. Always thinking the worst in people, especially me . . . that's what it seems like, anyway. He's real strict and old school, like 'children obey their parents no matter what' strict. My father *has* assaulted me many times, but not in the way you think. He calls me these horrible names, ones I don't like to think about." Hannah knew she wasn't going to tell him the skirt story. Even Deacon didn't need to know that gem of history. But suddenly, it all came into focus: "He tries to control me by shaming me."

Feeling dizzy, she stretched onto her back next to Deacon. "How can a father talk like that to his daughter? It's hard to forget the things he says. Those words, I torture myself with them, repeating them in my head over and over. Sometimes I just want the pain to go away . . . for *me* to go away." She looked into Deacon's eyes, searching for a trace of disgust or even boredom, but only saw tenderness. "I guess the LSD just magnified all those awful feelings to the point that I believed he was actually raping me."

Deacon reached for the side of Hannah's face, wiping her tear before it traveled into her earlobe. The sweet gesture made Hannah smile before she allowed herself to crumble. Like a tidal wave, she could feel the release, starting with her shoulders then moving down through her chest and arms and into her belly. Mercifully, Deacon did nothing to stop her. She shook the bed as she let her secret go.

———

Deacon held her for a while even after she stopped crying, stroking her hair and gently kissing her warm, wet face. Exhausted, Hannah felt wrung out but lighter. She exhaled, letting the unexpected sense of peace wash over her like a baptism and feeling suddenly fearless.

"Why do you deal, Deacon? It's not like you need the money, just look at this house." His body stiffened like a cadaver, but she didn't let it deter her. She rotated onto her side, propping herself up on her elbow, and waited.

After what seemed a small eternity, he finally answered. "Power," he said. "Believe it or not, I wasn't always cool, you know, like respected. As a little kid, I was beat up a lot. Dealing gave me power."

"But what if you get caught or . . . *expelled?*"

"Guess I'm willing to take that chance. Live on the edge, right?" Deacon pulled her on top of him. "Hey, let's do it on my parents' bed. Not like my dad ever sleeps there."

"Eww gross, no."

"Why not? It would be fun."

Hannah scanned his face to see if he was kidding, but he wasn't. First his dad's study and now this. "Do you *want* us to get caught or something? Does that turn you on?"

With a sudden jerk, Deacon rolled her off of him. He

turned away and swung his legs off the bed, grabbing his clothes off the floor.

"Hey wait, what's wrong?" she asked, but he'd already shut down. "So that's it? You don't like *my* questions? You can ask about my dad 'raping' me, for Christ's sake, but I can't ask about your hang-ups with your parents? Well, F you!"

Too pissed to think, Hannah felt her tears coming again. *What the hell just happened?* Feeling her nose fill up, she reached for the top drawer in the nightstand next to the bed.

"Don't!" he said, grabbing her wrist.

"What? I'm just looking for a tissue! What's your problem? Let me *go!*"

Without a word, he released his grip and threw the box of tissues on his bureau toward her. Then he sat back down on the bed, holding his head in his hands. Hannah blew her nose and began to get dressed. All she wanted to do was get the hell out of there.

Deacon cleared his throat. "This thing with my parents, it's so fucked up. I don't, like—really, it's nothing." Hannah watched him fumble with his words. He seemed unable to look at her, and his brown cheeks were growing redder by the moment. He thrust his leg into his jeans, shaking his head. The angrier he got, the smaller he became.

"What are you afraid of? Your parents never coming back for you?"

He shook his head. "Nah, I can't wait to finally get out of here and away from *them.*"

Hannah didn't buy it for a second, but this brought up new questions. "So what's going to happen to us? Next year you'll be going to school . . ."

"What, college?" He laughed. "I'm not going to college. Hell, my parents could get me in anywhere. One call from Kingsley . . . I guess I could deal on campus—again—but school's not for me. I'm better off alone. Always have been."

Alone. The word stung somewhere deep inside of her. What were they doing, then? She couldn't let it drop. "So we're having a fling, nothing too serious, right? Just sex, right Deacon?" Hannah finished dressing and threw open his bedroom door. She'd walk home; at this point, she didn't really care. *He used you. You mean nothing to him. You whore.*

"Please . . . *please* don't leave," he said quietly. She hesitated, and he came around to her back, placed his hands on her shaking shoulders. His touch blurred her anger and the jumbled mess in her head. With a long sigh, she reached up for his hands and he rested his chin on her head.

"All these mixed signals. I'm so confused. What exactly are we doing?"

"Just stay, please."

"So what's with that kid Toby? He's always hanging around. He came to my house last week looking for you," Hannah said. She was sitting on the counter in Deacon's palatial kitchen, watching him cut a roll to make her a sandwich. Every appliance and surface screamed state-of-the-art nouveau riche, and was so squeaky clean you could eat off of it— *Probably perform surgery,* she thought. Hannah wondered when Babette's cleaning crew came through. It was the complete opposite of her crusty kitchen.

"Yeah, he just transferred from another school . . . I think. He bought from me once . . . I can't shake him."

"He's infatuated with you," she teased.

Deacon's face clouded over again, and his knife beheaded the piece of bread like a guillotine.

"Hey, I'm just kidding! I never took you for a homophobe."

"Huh?"

"Never mind. It's just this kid's pretty intense. Calls you 'bro' all the time like he's your best friend—"

"He's not my brother!"

His defensive tone caught Hannah by surprise. "Of course not. Chill, Deacon. Geesh!" She jumped off the counter and swooped up half of the sandwich in her hand. "Come on, I gotta get home."

Deacon stared at the half she left for him, his eyes still somewhere else. "Yeah, coming." He picked up the knife, hovering the blade above the sandwich, and stabbed it.

CHAPTER 28

"SHE'S NOT YOUR DRUG BITCH TO PLAY WITH!" GILLIAN shouted. Deacon smiled condescendingly at her before turning his back. You could see her seething from a whole hallway away. It was the way her lower jaw jutted out with her top lip pulled back, exposing her venomous fangs. Her icepick stare was trying hard to puncture his smooth façade.

Hannah had heard them arguing from down the hall. Now, her curiosity chained her to the nearest water fountain. She wanted to hear more.

"Fuck you, Deacon," Gillian hissed, trying to regain his attention. "She's done, that's all. Leave her alone."

"She's a big girl, Gillian. Does what the fuck she wants," he said, now inches from her again, haughtily peering down at her.

The exchange reminded Hannah of Gillian's passionate kiss in the backyard with the pretty dark-haired girl. *She must really like this girl*, Hannah thought. How strange to see the meanest girl in school so crazed over someone. Hannah could see herself defending Deacon in the same way. But it was so much more complicated for them. She almost felt sorry for Gillian.

The cold fountain water made Hannah shiver, breaking her from her trance, and she began to stroll toward Deacon, blurring everyone out except for him. Their eyes locked, and Gillian was forgotten. His unwavering gaze in front of her nemesis made Hannah feel suddenly powerful. She'd never known such power.

"Hey," Deacon called out. Gillian swung around, hurling daggers at Hannah with every cruel cell in her body, but Hannah ignored her; she just floated into her boyfriend's arms and kissed him.

"Let's go," she said, wrapping her arm around him, fitting perfectly in the folds of his coat, beaming and content. She didn't say a word until they were halfway down the hall, but then she whispered, "So Gillian's girlfriend works for you?"

"Yeah, Jade. The girl in the park."

CHAPTER 29

"I KNOW YOU HAVE IT, BRO. I'M JUST ASKING THIS ONCE."

"Nah, I don't think so," Deacon said, shaking his head like he was blowing off a panhandler on the street. *What a fucking loser, get a life.*

"Why not . . . what's a few hundred out of *your* pocket?" Toby said, taking a step closer. They were back by the lockers in the short hallway at school, near the gymnasium where he'd first met Hannah.

"Listen, poser—show some respect. Unlike you, I *work* for my money . . . taking risks every day. You have no fricking clue!" Deacon felt his neck grow hotter just breathing the same air as this guy. He wanted to rip that annoying varsity letter right off of his jacket.

"I'll pay you back!" Toby said, his voice skyrocketing a few octaves too high.

"How?" But Deacon knew the answer even before Toby said it.

"I'll work for you, man. Whatever you need . . ."

Deacon always found ways to stay competitive in his line of work, creating new cravings for clients and reinforcing any old ones to keep them coming back. Dangling the candy, as they said. If his customers declined using needles, preferring to snort their heroin, Deacon would purposely put a needle in their bag anyway, telling them, "You're wasting your time the other way. With the money you're spending, you want to get the quickest, best possible high."

Deacon shrugged it off as a way of doing business, even when a client attempted to get clean. They would cave eventually and end up calling him; the need to get high was always more powerful than their resolve.

Jade's cousin worked in a hospital, so hermetically sealed needles were pretty easy to get for their little operation. Bobby didn't have as many connections as Jade, but his size came in handy for protection when a disgruntled client or unwanted outsider got out of hand. Toby's size would also make him a good bodyguard, but Deacon was never going to let Toby into his circle—at least not that way.

Deacon waited for the courtyard to clear out before making his call. Hannah's mother was taking her to a follow-up doctor's visit for her nose, even though she'd told her it felt fine. Standing in front of the payphone, he glanced back a couple of times at the table where he usually sat with Hannah, wishing she were here now. Then he dialed the old, familiar number, the one he used to prank incessantly as a kid and unfortunately still knew by heart.

"Yeah. I know . . . I know. Listen—thought we could work something out. Meet me tonight at eight thirty, Gossamer Park . . . under the lights. Yeah." Deacon hung up and dug his hand into his jeans for another quarter. "Yeah, hey, it's me," he said, jamming his other hand into his front pocket. He leaned in closer to the phone's kiosk, shielding himself from the November wind that was rummaging through his trench coat. "I'm going to need you to do me a favor, tonight . . . yeah . . . I'll explain when I see you, around 8:00 p.m. Good. And—you can't tell anyone . . . especially Gillian . . . just between us. Yeah . . . and oh, I need you to dress preppy again."

———

Toby showed up right on time, pulling up in the candy-red Camaro that always made Deacon's skin crawl. He could see the scene playing out in front of him: Toby getting the new set of wheels for his sixteenth birthday or something, his sweet, dear old dad dangling the keys in front of his face, both father and son beaming with pride. Hating him even more, Deacon traded his clenched jaw for a smile and continued with his plan.

"'Sup?" Deacon said, acknowledging Toby with a casual lift of the chin. The other boy mimicked the gesture back, but then he immediately began fidgeting as if the bottom of his feet were on fire. Ignoring him, Deacon furrowed his brow and zeroed in on something past Toby's shoulder in the distance. Toby turned his head.

"Well, I guess your little lady couldn't wait. Here she is now."

The chilly night air flowed thickly around the tall oak trees and park lamps, making it difficult to see her features fully through the fog, but there was the slender body, the long hair pulled back in that ever-present headband.

Deacon smiled, watching Toby's beady eyes start to blink

rapidly. He pulled a pipe and lighter from his trench coat and began to speak to Toby like he was a child, sweet and steady. "If you're going to work for me, you're going to have to have a go . . . just this once, of course." He motioned the pipe toward him, concealing his contempt in the shadows.

"You'll front me the money then?"

"Of course," Deacon said, already seeing the end in sight. It was all going to happen, and at his own hands; he felt wonderfully wicked and just. *Here's to you, Dad.*

"Not here, out in the open. I don't want Taylor to see me."

"Turn away then, keep it low," Deacon gently coaxed.

Toby took the pipe and lighter out of his hands. His palm shook waiting for Deacon to drop the rock into the pipe, and sweat bubbled across his brow as he fumbled with the lighter, unable to get it to light. He turned away and just about dropped the pipe, before Deacon caught them both.

"I–I don't know, man. I don't think I can do it."

"Try."

Toby shook his head, and tears came from the corner of his eyes. He glanced back at the girl waiting in the fog then to Deacon again.

"I can't, bro. Please . . . please don't make me—"

"Everyone who works for me—listen. You're the one who needed the cash so badly. Do this for me; I need to see your level of loyalty. I've got the money on me." Deacon was still holding the pipe and lighter under Toby's face, just waiting for the virgin to inhale.

"I can't," Toby said, jerking his head back, fear lighting up his eyes as they nervously darted from Deacon's face then back to the girl coming through the fog. Toby took a of couple steps backward, nearly tripping over his feet, before he turned and tore off toward his car. "T–Taylor, I–I–I've got to go . . . I'll call you later!"

Jade stopped walking and nodded, offering a flimsy wave. Toby peeled out of the parking lot without looking back.

Deacon kicked the ground, exasperated, manically walking around in a circle, clenching and unclenching his fists. He'd punch a wall if there were one. *Fucking waste of time. Pussy.*

Jade finally emerged from the shadows in her over-the-top preppy ensemble, causing Deacon to laugh heartily for the first time in a long time.

"Nice job," he said, composing himself.

She yanked the headband off her head, rolled her eyes at him, and eagerly took the glass pipe from his hands.

CHAPTER 30

1966

SWALLOW ASPIRIN 4X A DAY. *CHECK.*

Smoke incessantly. *Check.*

Drink Dong Quai or Raspberry Leaf tea. *Check. Check.*

Take exorbitant amounts of vitamin C for two weeks. *Check.*

Raise arms overhead whenever possible. *Check.*

Jump from the top of the stairs. *Check.*

Still Babette's belly grew.

The "fall" from the top of the winding staircase was by far her best effort. Kingsley patted his young wife's head and called her clumsy that day. She hid the unwanted pregnancy from everyone, especially from the man she was growing to detest more by the minute. She'd had affairs herself, of course; but at the end of the day, she had to keep up the pretense, that ghastly arrangement she'd made with her father, who had promised to leave her alone for once in return.

But after she married, her preppy playboys had lost interest. Even the string of pool boys, the tennis pros, and the stately gentleman in the black suit who polished the silver once a month couldn't keep up with Babette's appetite. Eventually, she grew bored, and she sent her stallions to the glue factory for poor dressage and showing.

When her period didn't come those first few months, Babette brushed it off like everything else. After all, they were never going to have a family. That was certain. But when she didn't bleed in her fifth month, her worry spread like an unreachable itch. Five plastic sticks later, she knew no reputable doctor would give her an abortion this late in the game. There had to be another way.

Babette set off into the city's Chinatown area to see a renowned mystic she'd heard about through her ladies' teas. The acclaimed sorcerer owned a shop—part opium den, hidden away and annoyingly hard to find—that specialized in "female issues."

Babette was already out of breath when she reached the squat storefront. She wiped her brow with a monogrammed handkerchief and surveyed her surroundings. The place looked more like a forgotten grocery than opium den. Black vertical bars donned its cracked, newspaper-covered windows, along with a partially lit hanging neon sign for Chinese beer and cigarettes that buzzed like a horde of dung beetles. No tinkling of bells welcomed her as she stepped over its threshold. Instead, she was met with a vacuum of silence and a hanging cloud of sweet-smelling dust that immediately made her cough.

In the far corner, a young woman stood bent over a magazine atop a long glass counter filled with stacks of Asian newspapers. She busily snapped her gum, ignoring Babette's presence. The girl's hair was shaved to a finger's length on either side around her ears, while long, spiked, jet black and electric blue tips fanned the center like a rooster. Her guarded eyes were rimmed in thick black kohl, her thin lips painted blue. To Babette, it was obvious that the girl dabbled in street drugs and was part of that new punk scene she'd read about in the *Times. Some mystic*, she thought.

She cleared her throat. "Hello?"

The girl disappeared into a back room through a doorway covered with long, flowing, floor-length silk curtains embroidered with green, gold, and black dragons, that swooshed seemingly on their own from side to side. Babette heard her speak in clipped, harsh commands. Then there was nothing. Babette began turning her wedding band with her left thumb, making small circles. *One, two, three, four, five.* She moved on to checking the backs of her earrings—*one, two, three, four, five*—and straightening the strands of necklaces over her suit—*one, two, three, four, five.* She had just started the sequence again when the girl returned to the counter; with a great flourish, the silk curtains parted, making the dragons resume their dance. The surly punk-rock girl suddenly became the least of Babette's worries.

More male than female in appearance, the androgynous mystic blinked soft, clouded eyes that made Babette wonder if she were blind. Her shrunken-apple smile exposed large gaps in her teeth, while her head vibrated off her pencil neck like a jack-in-the-box. Her round, curious face spawned wiry black hairs that started at her brows, snaked through her nostrils, and mottled her pruned chin like a stubbly beard. Compounding her diminutive stature, her back was stooped and twisted by an abnormal protruding curvature, perhaps from birth, that had frozen her in a continuous bow. Babette forced herself to keep her focus on the old woman's face and not the thing that seemed to be following her.

It was evident that the elderly woman wasn't going to speak English, even if she knew any. Punk-rock girl reluctantly introduced herself simply as Wei, her granddaughter, and began translating the many ways their ancient sisters before them had performed natural miscarriages. The young girl's articulate speech surprised Babette, who raised her initial assessment of the girl to at least college-educated. *Probably a state school.*

Within minutes, Babette had purchased all of the recommended teas and herbs, along with an illustrated pamphlet, written in English, providing the step-by-step guidelines to handling unwanted pregnancies.

Relieved, Babette nodded and smiled politely at the mystic. She was closing her purse to leave when Wei suddenly stopped her.

"My grandmother would like to examine the baby."

What?

With surprising ease and agility, the mystic traveled around to the front of the counter and placed her T-Rex claws on either side of Babette's belly. The baby kicked wildly at her touch, delivering Babette a surprising amount of pain.

The old woman closed her eyes, and her face stilled, along with the baby's movements. After several long breaths, she spoke, looking into Babette's eyes as she did.

"My grandmother says you're too far along. This baby will be born."

Shit, shit.

"And that he already knows."

He? "I'm sorry, what does *he* know?" cried Babette.

"He knows that he's not wanted."

Jumping from the stairs happened nearly a week later, after a few too many bourbons and what was probably her millionth self-pity cry. She was praying to just die already rather than become someone's mother. Her own mother was so horrid—why would anyone ever aspire to that? It was bad enough growing up with the burden of being the child of a woman who had killed herself, her mother's shame forever scarring her life.

Still the baby grew. As did her hate.

"Is it mine?" asked Kingsley, looking forlorn and confused the night she finally told him. Babette had knocked on his study door after downing two highballs with very little ice. She was sort of hoping he'd take care of the thing once it came out. Wet nurses, nannies, and au pairs, whatever it took. She would be out of the country by then. European playboys could keep her amused for a while.

"Afraid so," Babette said, knowing she'd ridden all of her other horses with Trojans.

"Goddammit!"

"Yep."

CHAPTER 31

december 1989

"HEY THERE!" SHE SAID, SURPRISED AT HER OWN EXUBERANCE. She had waited most of the day to call him, rehearsing different scenarios in her head.

"Hi." He sounded sleepy, but at least she'd caught him at home.

"So your birthday's Saturday, right?"

"I guess?" Hannah could hear the smile in his voice.

"Well, I'd like to see you that day, celebrate a little, maybe?"

"Yeah, sure. I'll pick you up." He didn't sound overly excited, but at least he was willing. "I'd like to see you."

"You would?" she teased, feeling her heart sing.

"A lot."

Hannah convinced her mother to drive her to the grocery store the following Saturday morning so she could buy Deacon a birthday card and some flowers. They were meeting later at the library and then heading back to his house to be alone. She hadn't told her mom what she was getting or for whom, because they hadn't discussed Deacon since the time she saw them kissing outside their house. Even with all of the late-night calls and Hannah dragging the downstairs phone into her bedroom, neither of her parents had asked her about it. Maybe they were just relieved that she finally had a friend.

Hannah's mother already had an order waiting at the pharmacy, so it wasn't too hard to persuade her to go to the store. Alone in the greeting card aisle, Hannah giggled picking something out for Deacon, staying away from anything that seemed too mushy or made it look like she was trying too hard. The flowers were easier. She knew exactly what kind to get, and she couldn't wait to see the look on Deacon's face when she gave them to him. *It's what a girlfriend does for her boyfriend,* she thought, laughing to herself.

Driving home, Hannah noticed her name across the top of the paper prescription bag next to her on the seat. "What's this, Mom?" She glanced over at her mom's profile and her tight-knuckled grip on the steering wheel. Her eyes appeared sunken inside her sharp cheekbones, making her look older. Maybe she was dieting again—not like she needed to—or maybe she was still worrying about Kerry. "Mom?"

"What?" her mother answered sounding distracted. Hannah realized she was driving faster than normal. Instinctively, she placed one hand on the dashboard to brace herself.

"What's this?" Hannah motioned to the bag just as her mother slammed on the brakes, narrowly missing the car turning in front of them. Both of their heads catapulted forward, then snapped back and hit their headrests.

"Dr. Kittleman refilled your painkillers," her mom said, moving the car forward like nothing had happened.

"Why? It's not like I need them anymore."

"You ungrateful bitch," her mother said under her breath. "I got them for you in case you needed them, so you wouldn't wake in the middle of the night from the pain."

"When have I ever done that?"

"*Leave it, Hannah.*"

Hannah closed her eyes, feeling the familiar sharpness inside the top of her ribcage. The ache rolled over then traveled down her right arm into her thumb. *I never want to be with somebody who makes me feel this. Never*, she swore.

———

Hannah carefully pulled out the red roses, along with Deacon's card, from her book bag. She propped them up across his pillows in the center of the bed. They looked perfect. All she had to do was write something in the card before he got upstairs. She'd been toying with whether or not to sign it with the "L" word. Things had been really amazing between them lately, but he hadn't said it yet.

Hannah opened the drawer in his nightstand, looking for a pen. She pushed aside a torn piece of a Blow Pops box top with writing scribbled on the inside—when her hand jerked back like she'd touched something hot. Her mouth grew dry, and her blood began to pulse in her ears. Whatever she'd eaten earlier now polluted her mouth. Her hand shook lifting the first Polaroid from the drawer, then another one, followed by another. Thinking at first they were pictures of an ex-girlfriend, she gasped when she recognized her outfit and those boots—the first and last time she ever wore them.

She wanted to scream, scratch his eyes out, but she couldn't make a sound. She forced herself not to look away. Each of them depicted her lying on her back in her bedroom with her hands inside her clothing, grabbing herself. Hannah shuddered at the last one—the most disgusting of the three—which showed her finger in her mouth, her pants zipped down, and her legs spread.

That bastard posed me! But why?

Her stomach dropped recalling Deacon's "brotherly" way that weekend, how he'd helped her clean up and dispose of her incriminating bloodstained clothes and dirty rags. *Stupid, stupid girl!* Her head swiveled, and she spotted the camera on his bureau. She hadn't noticed it until now. She lunged and threw it against the wall. Wildly, she looked around the sparse room for more. She started pulling apart the roses, ripping off their heads. *Stupid, stupid girl!* The tiny thorns ripped through her hands, sending blood trickling down her arms and pooling inside her elbows. She felt none of it.

How many people have seen these photos? How far did he take it?

"It wasn't an accident. It was all planned!" she screamed, attempting to rip the pictures and then, when that proved hopeless, crumbling them in a ball. Blindly, she began throwing whatever was in her way. Her bloodied hands flew to her face, and she dug her nails in deep before a wave of cool air from the hallway hit her back. She could feel him there. She glared back with everything she had, not caring how she looked or what she'd done to his room.

His lips contorted as he spoke. "I took them when I

didn't know you. I was afraid you were going to rat me out. I thought I needed them, just in case. Hannah, please"—he tried to stop her from leaving the room, grabbing her shoulders—"I should have destroyed them after we got closer. I wanted to but . . . I liked looking at them."

"You're disgusting! Don't touch me . . . don't!"

"Please, Hannah. Don't leave."

Hannah flew down the mansion's long, winding staircase, frantically trying to remember the quickest way out. She swung open one of the large front doors, and the crack of the lion doorknocker rang out as if to say, *Told you so.*

She looked back. He wasn't coming after her.

She took off down the snowy hill from his house knowing she probably looked like a freak show, considering she never ran anywhere. Out of nowhere, her boot caught on a sheet of ice, sending her down hard on her butt. She tumbled several times, only coming to a stop when she plowed into a snowdrift. A dog started yelping from inside a neighbor's house. She slowly picked herself up, shaking off the snow caked from her hair down to her cold feet, stomping the ground until the tears came. She prayed that no one had seen her, especially him, and took the rest of the way down the hill more tentatively. *Moron.*

Wet and shivering, she walked home trailed by the awful memory of the time her father kicked her out of the car. *When will you ever learn*, the voice inside yelled. Hannah gritted her teeth. *Shit.* She'd left her book bag at his house. There was no way she was going back. She kept moving, trying not to cry, while the wind picked up, taunting her and her relentless stupidity. She cursed herself for believing the fairy tale—the one where the oh-so-cute, popular boy fell for the unlikely misfit, taking away her misery. Her chest felt like he'd carved something out of it with a jagged, dull knife, leaving her hollow and grotesque. She punched one leg hard, then the other one. *What a joke.* Believing that Deacon Giroux actually elevated her somehow by liking her, sleeping with her, even. *God, I'm no better than Taylor.*

She was about three miles out from her house when an old, green, two-door Chevrolet pulled up next to her. She ungracefully crossed the icy street to steer clear of whoever was driving it. She could hear its non-muffled engine sputtering along in the cold, its tires crunching the blackened snow. She picked up her pace, still avoiding eye contact.

"Hannah!"

Peter. She looked over at the car and shook her head. The last thing she wanted to do was explain.

"Come on, I'll take you home."

She thought about how much farther she had to go, and her resolve disappeared. "Thanks," she mumbled, lowering her head and getting into the car. "You have a car?"

"It's my parents'. I get to drive it when they don't need it for work."

The cranked heat hit her numb face immediately, along with the upholstery's old potato smell. Within minutes her feet and hands started to thaw; it hurt, like razors were slicing her skin, but it was a comfort not to talk or feel the need to fill in the silence. Peter always seemed to give her that space.

When they arrived at her house, Hannah mustered a small smile. "Thanks," she said again before shutting the car door.

CHAPTER 32

Deacon all but vanished after the blow-up over the Polaroids. Hannah didn't see him at school and he never came by her house, except when she found her book bag on her porch the next morning. Toby kept coming around, though, hammering her about Deacon's whereabouts. She now understood how annoying the kid could be. He seemed so desperate and clueless at the same time. After a while, he finally got the hint—like the rest of the school, judging by their knowing looks—that she and Deacon had broken up.

Somehow, she held it together in front of all of them as she numbly walked around school, even though she felt like a pyramid of cards ready to collapse at the first whisper of wind. The loneliness of being without him weighed heavily on everything she did. Seeing him leaning against her locker between classes or walking the halls with his arm around her—those were the moments she missed the most. Those moments and their friendship. Beyond being incredibly attracted to him, she longed for the friend she thought she'd had.

The routine of school helped, but the everything-is-fine charade was exhausting. Every evening, she released the pain inside her bedroom walls, howling into her pillow and rocking her stuffed hippo until she wore herself out and slept. When she wasn't ranting in her diary about the million things she wanted to tell Deacon, she tortured herself listening to the songs they'd shared, including the night she'd been "his girl" at the Halloween party and the day they spent at his house, mostly in his bed. Each song stabbed a different part of her.

Deacon's sudden abandonment only fueled Hannah's fear that he'd been using her. Still, she didn't understand how he could be so cruel. Peter had tried to warn her. But Hannah knew she'd just wanted to believe someone actually cared for her—loved her, even.

It doesn't matter, she told herself; somehow, she'd survive this. And at least life without Deacon meant being free of the constant worry of his drug-dealing world pulling her down with him. But what about those pictures—what was he going to do with them? Part of her wanted to believe what he'd said, but still, he'd been a monster. Giving her that powerful drug then taking advantage of her and posing her like some nympho. She shuddered at how free she'd been with him. *Slut. Whore.* She pushed the words down again, growing sadder with every passing day—and stepping closer to the belief that he'd been laughing at her this whole time.

CHAPTER 33

The hallways emptied as Gillian headed to her locker, ignoring the bell for seventh period. She checked her Swatch, wondering if she had enough time to get to Jade's school before dismissal. She pushed aside the nagging feeling that her girlfriend was pulling away, creating a chasm between them that felt less and less reparable. If things weren't complicated enough, this unaccustomed sense of desperation piqued Gillian to no end. *I have to stay focused*, she told herself. She had to hit first before they came after her. They couldn't find out. Ever.

Ugh, there's that skank again. Gillian had to resist the urge to wring Hannah's neck every time she saw her, like now—at least until she could figure out what to do about her. She knew Taylor could be coerced into helping, as could her stupid boyfriend, Toby, the latest flavor of the month. But Taylor was acting weird lately—distracted. Then there was ever-driven Leeza and her nauseating quest to get elected Queen of Hearts at the upcoming winter formal. Leeza went on incessantly about it over lunch, especially how great it would look on her college applications, while Gillian surreptitiously rolled her eyes and kicked Taylor under the table.

What lit Leeza's fire to try and get ahead in life meant

nothing to Gillian; she just didn't see the point. Besides, her best friend was never going to survive her biggest secret, the one Leeza had blurted out after too many Bartles & Jaymes wine coolers one night. The Leeza-lites—Gillian's pet name for Leeza's parents—were secretly broke and had been for a while. Like, straight off of Walton's Mountain broke. Gillian snickered at the thought of Leeza's social-climbing parents, the biggest wannabes in town, the couple who always found endless ways to flaunt their "decorator showcase" of a home and two leased sports cars in the driveway, now suffocating under a pile of debt and a please-don't-tell-anyone pending home foreclosure. What a bunch of *posers*. Gillian sniffed. She wouldn't be able to hold on to Leeza's secret for long.

She cocked an eyebrow, taking in the familiar dark figure coming down the hall, and grabbed her chance to play. "I see you're back," she sneered, giving Deacon the once-over and wondering how far she could push him. Jade's involvement in Deacon's operation had always irked her big time, and now she was using. Her girlfriend was pulling away, and Gillian wasn't going down without turning it into a blood bath. Deacon or Hannah—someone was going to pay for Jade's new craving.

Deacon said nothing, just kept walking toward the glass exit doors. His hunched shoulders and fisted hands gave him the appearance of a captive lion, and his bloodshot eyes and ashen face made him look like he hadn't slept in a week.

"Why do you care about that little *skank*? She's just another notch—"

He smashed a fist into one of the doors, nearly shattering the glass. "Shut up, Gillian," he snarled. "You have no idea."

CHAPTER 34

1972–1981

"WE'RE GOING ON A LITTLE TRIP, DEAR."

"Will we be gone for long?"

"Yes."

"But why?" Deacon could feel his lips begin to quiver. Once again, he tried so hard to be the tough guy like his father had taught him—"No tears, never any tears," he'd scold his six-year-old son—but Deacon didn't want to leave; he wanted to find out who that little boy in his father's arms had been days earlier. The one that had made his father look so different. He'd never seen him look like that before, like the fathers on TV.

Deacon could tell his mom was getting annoyed. She was already twisting and re-twisting her pearls, her thin lips silently counting to five. Never a good sign. He couldn't seem to please her, either.

"Mommy, I want to go back home! Please let me stay!" Deacon began to cry. He sat on the floor, refusing to sit next to her, but he grabbed onto her leg like a security blanket when the town car began to pull away from the house. Panic rose up inside his throat. *Wait! Where's Daddy, why isn't he coming for me?* Desperate, he started to thrash about, pounding the back of the front seat, but both the driver and his mother ignored his tantrum.

The big trees were getting farther away. He had to do something. *Now.*

He dug his fingernails into his mother's fleshy calf, ripping her sheer, nude-colored pantyhose and bringing up red droplets that started heading for her Halston heel. She gasped and kicked her son off of her. Deacon's head hit the window, causing the driver to glare at him over his shoulder, before he slid back onto the floor, dumbstruck, his head throbbing. He touched a hand to his face and was momentarily transfixed by the red stickiness on his fingertips. Then he wept, silently but hard, yearning to fall through the car's vibrating floorboards. His chest ached for his father, his home, his toys, and especially his blue bedroom with the glowing stars on the ceiling—convinced he'd never see them again.

There they are again. Deacon crouched behind the park dumpster, waiting for the five of them to leave—the same kids who'd been torturing him ever since he arrived at his grandfather's estate nearly 730 days ago. Not like he was counting. For some reason, they'd come back. Probably to mess with him more.

Deacon bit into his lip, grimacing and holding his crotch. His front teeth sank down further, bringing up a salty iron taste. He couldn't take it; he bolted over to the park bathroom, praying the other boys wouldn't see him. He leaned back with all his might to pull open the heavy men's room door, then ran to the nearest stall and gratefully gave in to the bottle of Coke he'd drunk an hour earlier.

His eyes snapped at the sound of someone running the faucet outside the stall door. Was it one of the bullies? He panicked, clenching his butt cheeks until he heard whomever it was singing a jumbled rendition of "Sweet Home Alabama." He knew then it was someone else. *Someone older*.

He sucked in his breath before exiting the stall. When he got to the bathroom door, he glanced back at the skinny teen washing his hands. The stranger smiled at him, revealing a toothy, horse-like grin above his "Led Zeppelin America" T-shirt and black leather vest. A chrome chain wallet bulged from his Levi's.

You could hear Jack singing before you ever saw him coming; he was always belting out a cacophonic repertoire, regardless of who was listening. His teeth, yellow from his chain-smoking, made him appear years older than seventeen, and when he smiled, it looked like a snarl. Still, the park kids flocked to his side to hear his animated, often hilarious rant about some new band or movie. The charismatic teen soon commanded the park, speaking in a soft manner that made all of the kids take notice, even the rough ones—and most of all, Deacon. And Jack didn't seem to mind him following him around.

"It's getting dark," he said one night. "Where are your parents, Little D?"

"I live with my grandfather," Deacon said, jumping off the top of the picnic table where Jack was smoking.

"Where's he at?"

Deacon shrugged. "Someone else is supposed to watch me," he said, kicking a rock.

"Like a babysitter?"

"Sort of."

"Where are *they?*"

Deacon shrugged again and searched for more rocks to kick.

"Are you *rich* or something?"

"No."

"I kinda think you are. Ya go to school?"

"Doesn't everybody?"

"No, not everybody." Jack looked away then. "Ya like school?"

"Not much . . . well, just swim team. But that's after school."

"Ahh, a swimmer . . . I can see that."

"Shut up."

"Do you wear those little *banana hammocks?*" Jack snorted.

Without thinking, Deacon hurled a rock over his head.

"Watch it, you little fucker!" He grabbed Deacon by the back of his jeans, lifting him off the ground.

"Put me down . . . put me down!" Deacon cried.

Jack yanked him up a few more times before finally releasing him. Deacon spun around and charged at him headfirst. Jack grabbed Deacon's wrists while he fruitlessly fought. The more Jack laughed at the boy's efforts, the more Deacon's fury grew, until finally the tears sprung like an uncorked dam, eventually drowning him. He collapsed to the ground and buried his head in the crook of his arm.

Jack lit up another cigarette, wearing one of his snarling smiles, and picked some small pieces of tobacco from between his teeth. "Wanna shoot hoops?"

"Yeah," Deacon said, wiping his nose onto his shirtsleeve. He grabbed the ball from Jack's hands and took off toward the courts.

———

Late one night, Jack lit up another type of cigarette—one that was creased and twisted tightly at either end, more like a large worm than one of his Marlboros. He inhaled it differently too, maximizing his intake and holding it for several seconds before exhaling. It released a sharp sweet smell that made Jack's eyes sparkle.

Jack had shared other cigarettes with him, so immediately, Deacon asked for a turn. He tried to imitate the cool, easy way he saw Jack do it, but instead it burned his throat and he coughed like crazy.

"That's okay, little man." Jack laughed gently and his top lip peeled back, revealing his gums. "There will be time enough for that."

"Nah, I can do it, really," Deacon said.

Jack took another hit and held in the smoke, his eyes widening. "You know what would really piss off your grandfather, that fucker? Hmm, I've got a novel idea. Is that cool— if we try a little experiment?"

"Sure, I guess."

"It's a package I need delivered. Let me write down the address." Jack ripped off a piece of a cardboard Blow Pops box from a nearby garbage can and scrawled the information on the inside. "Now, I'm trusting you, Little D—don't let me down."

"You want me to go *now?*" Deacon asked, looking at the darkening sky.

———

Deacon's heart hammered nails into his chest as his little legs frantically pedaled his candy-red Schwinn Deluxe Stingray—the coveted bike all the kids wanted, with chrome fenders, a bucket banana seat, and wide handlebars, complete with sissy bar shock suspension—down the sidewalk. This probably wasn't the use his mother had in mind when she sent the bike from Europe as a Christmas present.

Deacon kept rechecking the address on the cardboard box top he'd wrapped around his right handlebar. He was worried he'd never find the place. But when he heard the music and saw the clouds of billowing smoke from the apartment building's third-floor windows, he understood what Jack had meant when he said he couldn't miss the "party scene."

Deacon took the flights two steps at a time before reaching the door, which was vibrating from the music blasting behind it. He knocked and waited for a minute. Impatiently, he rapped again—this time more loudly, using his fist—until the door swung open and a young, pretty redhead in a green bandana and brown suede fringe vest with nothing much underneath appeared.

"Jesus, what do we have here? Hey, little man, what's your name?" She crouched down to make them eye level and started to pull him into the party like he was a toy.

"Stop it! Stop it!" Deacon wailed. "I'm here to see Gunther."

He wiggled out from underneath her grip. Her hands felt sweaty and hot, and worse, she reeked of beer and stinky cheese.

"Come here, little boy, don't you want Maggie to give you a kiss?" She grabbed his hand and slid it inside her vest, rubbing it across her hard nipple. "Doesn't that feel good? Bet you never touched a girl before—"

"Stop it, Maggie, leave the kid alone." A tall, rangy man pushed her aside, and the party absorbed her back into the chaos. Deacon's rescuer resembled more of a caveman than a human, with black snarly hair that hung past his shoulders and a long, scraggly beard, the longest Deacon had ever seen. He wore dark round sunglasses and purple bellbottoms without a shirt, and lots of beaded necklaces flapped over his tan, round belly.

"I-I, I'm here to see Gunther," Deacon stammered, scared he would pee his pants.

"That'd be me."

"Here," Deacon said shyly, without looking up. He thrust the small package into the man's hand and took off down the stairs. He was nearly at the bottom when the guy started shouting. Deacon froze, unsure what to do next.

"You forgot the dough," the man yelled to him. Shaking his head at his stupidity, Deacon walked back, more confidently this time.

"Take it, kid," the guy said and handed him a wad of cash before slamming the door.

Deacon had never seen so much money before. Pedaling back, he felt alive, filled with a mixture of pride and relief. He practically flung himself into Jack's arms back at the park, the money gripped tightly in his hands.

"Good job, Little D, good job." Jack beamed as he counted every curled, damp bill.

That night, Deacon placed the Blow Pops box top underneath his pillow, along with the five-dollar bill Jack gave him, too stoked to even sleep.

Deacon learned the trade fast, running Jack's errands, occasionally encountering grown-up situations that he always managed to sidestep unscathed, keeping a low profile and remaining undetected by the cops.

"You're like Teflon, Little D—nothing sticks to you!" Jack would crow.

By age twelve, Deacon had become a full-fledged dealer, a partner in Jack's growing territory. Thanks to his cute, clean-cut looks, he fit in with the upper-crust clients and could deal to wealthier circles, ones that had eluded Jack before.

When Deacon's grandfather pushed to send him to a prestigious boys' prep school in Massachusetts, it was Jack who saw it as an ideal opportunity for him to get into all those rich kids' pockets—creating customers on his mean old grandfather's dime. Deacon put on a good face, but inside he still felt like that kid hiding behind the park dumpster.

At first, it wasn't so bad. When the older kids at the new school discovered that the precocious twelve-year-old could supply their weekend parties with just about anything they wanted, they soon invited him everywhere, treating Deacon like their new best friend. It was fun to be so popular, even though they didn't hang or talk with him the way Jack did. Meeting girls and getting teachers to overlook his late homework and struggling grades also got easier. But best of all, Deacon's business grew; rich prep-school boys apparently came with an endless supply of cash. In just two years, he nearly tripled the business he had done in his four years with Jack. Still, Deacon never escaped the sadness that crept inside his chest late at night when he was alone in his bed, or when he saw the other boys still getting care packages of goodies and notes from their parents.

"Hey D, how come *you* don't ever get anything?" Thomas, a fellow classmate with a crooked smile whose father owned some big commercial transport business, asked him over lunch in the Dining Hall one day. The boisterous table, lined with teens in navy blue blazers with a gold-embroidered school crest on the pocket, suddenly went hush, all eyes riveted and waiting. Deacon had an audience.

He slowly loosened his uniform tie away from his neck, his smirk spreading into one of his wide, handsome smiles. "I don't need that sissy crap . . . I'm a self-made man," he said haughtily, enjoying the look of awe in their eyes. "Besides, what I can get you is sooo much better. Real candy, you hear what I'm saying?"

"Speaking of . . ." Thomas interjected, tipping his head in the direction of the new kid at school. He'd arrived just days earlier. The table all turned, checking out the guy walking into the dining hall. The kid looked lost and a bit dorky in a nervous sort of way. He was built like an athlete, with wide shoulders and stocky legs, and appeared as dimwitted as they come. Deacon bit into the side of his cheek as he eyed the new classmate. He shook his head and grinned; he'd groom him into a customer in no time.

A couple of weeks later, Deacon was walking with the new kid back to the dorms when he noticed a hunter-green Jaguar convertible coming up the campus's main drive. Like a flash from a camera, Deacon's memory of sitting on top of his father's lap and steering down their long driveway flooded his brain, disorientating him until he could blink away the floating spots and refocus. *What in the world is he doing here?* Deacon's veins flowed—first with a rush of excitement, then by an old sense of queasiness. He kept squinting to get a better look. *God, what am I going to say?* His mind spun wildly.

"Listen ... Toby, right? There's something I need to do—"

But Toby kept walking, oblivious to him and waving to the car coming to a stop. Deacon froze. A cold, creepy feeling crawled up his neck. He quickly moved behind one of the buildings. *Don't look. Dammit, don't look. Shit.* Deacon stepped out in time to see his father's face light up when he high-fived Toby. Then a private handshake commenced, full of fist bumps and waving gestures that ripped Deacon's heart out, rolling it onto the cement and stomping on it until it stopped beating.

Babette and her white limo appeared at school the following week. They were flying home. To his *real* home. His grandfather had dictated his marching orders to him the day before over the phone, something about the need to reassemble the family due to the fact that Kingsley's promising political career had never been hotter and his Grandfather Pierre needed some fresh "plastic" connections.

His family was reeling him back because he could be useful. And he was their captive. Absently, he began stroking the circular scar inside his left palm. He could see the lit cigar hanging out of the old man's mouth by the way he spoke. He shuddered, remembering what burned flesh smelled like. All at once, he was six again and hiding, always hiding. He kept his eyes closed long after his grandfather hung up, imagining himself alone in a vast, black ocean, treading water just before a massive wave engulfed him.

When she arrived, Babette looked years younger than she had the last time he saw her. She gave him one of her tight smiles, which seemed even more taut from the evident "work" that had been done, but little else. All the things he'd planned to say to his mother fell away within minutes during that car ride to the airport, solidifying his own cowardice. In its place, a grotesque weed grew, masked in their polite silence, as he breathed the same air as the woman who had abandoned him nearly nine years earlier.

CHAPTER 35

december 1989

"MOM? MOM? WAKE UP, MOM! MOMMY?"

Hannah had come in the kitchen for a snack after school. She'd spotted the manicured talons first, reaching across the linoleum floor; then her mother's arm jutting out from the bottom of the counter, frozen and bent like one of Kerry's dirty baby dolls. Hannah lunged for her blindly. Her school bag and kneecaps smacked the floor just as the room pulled out from underneath her. She began rocking, as if in prayer, over her mother's lifeless body. "No, Mommy! Wake up, wake up!"

She got enough of a hold of herself to take action. "The phone—where's the damn phone?" she shouted. She followed the phone cord around the house, smacking herself into the wall, until she found the receiver lying on the ground. Crazily, she dialed 911—then dropped the receiver. She took a big breath and commanded herself to calm down. Then, out of the corner of her eye, she saw them: Kerry's little legs dangling from the corduroy couch, her fleeced Droge bear clutched at her side, her eyes glazed like an ice rink.

"Oh my god, Kerry! What did you *do?*" Hannah's head spun around frantically, searching the living room for something she didn't want to find. "You're just coked up on Fruit Loops, right Kerry girl? Nothing . . . more . . ." Then she saw the empty pill bottle on the floor. *Childproof caps my ass!*

"Shit, shit! Think, dammit, think," Hannah cried into the phone.

"911 operator, what is the nature of your emergency?"

Hannah took a deep breath.

She stayed on the line with the operator until the ambulance arrived, long enough for her to hallucinate leaving her body and floating upward, hovering over her mother's sprawled body then traveling over her little sister's limp form just a few feet away. She imagined the three of them dead while she waited for their spirits to join her mid-flight.

———

She stuck her head outside her bedroom, listening for sounds downstairs and from the floor above. She stepped warily into the hallway. Her head felt warped from crying so much, but she could still hear the starburst wall clock in the kitchen ticking like a drippy faucet. The house suddenly breathed differently now that her mom and Kerry were gone.

Hannah had locked herself in her room that afternoon after going to see them in that facility—a cold, antiseptic institution meant for crazy people, not her mom and sister. She shook her head as if it were an Etch-A-Sketch, hoping to erase the vivid picture of them lying on those cots with their eyes closed, wearing paper gowns and covered by a starched white sheet. The whole time she was there, she'd worried that the annoyingly affable staff would pull the sheet over each of their heads once she left. *Please, God, no.*

Her stomach growled just as she switched on the kitchen light. She wondered if she'd find something in the fridge that wasn't expired.

"Oh!" Her legs wobbled at the sight of her father sitting at the table, sucking the oxygen from the room. "Sorry, I didn't know anyone was here." She began to turn back, but then heard a small, asthmatic-sounding breath escape from his lips.

"Your mother, she sort of checked out when you were born," said a weary voice that didn't belong to her father.

"What?" Hannah stopped short, confusing his meaning, thinking her mother was somehow already checking out of the facility.

"His name was Michael . . . he came just a year before you were born," he said slowly, looking down at his palms then flipping them over, inspecting them. A brief smile touched his lips when he lifted his head, reminding Hannah of her parents' wedding picture, which made them both looked so young and carefree. "He was just beautiful, we were over the moon about him." Her father's hands started skimming the table, smoothing down a tablecloth that wasn't there.

"First-time parents, we were so nervous, trying to do everything right . . ." His hands stopped moving. The smile extinguished.

Hannah brought a hand to her chest and held her breath.

"Your mother found him that morning . . . blue . . . not even a week . . ." His breath caught before his face collapsed onto itself and he turned from her.

Hannah cupped her hands over her mouth. She could see it all so clearly, and it hurt.

"They told us he'd been born with a heart defect." The last word hung in the air. It sounded so small and innocent, not like something that could kill a baby.

He let out an odd laugh, and Hannah wondered if he'd been drinking. "It sounds morbid now, but your mom used to dress you in his clothes like you were her little prince. Drawers of clothes she'd gotten from baby showers . . . family . . ." He tucked his chin into his chest. "Your mom blamed herself. Thinking if only she'd checked on him sooner, just maybe . . . It didn't matter what they told us. Our beautiful boy . . ."

"So, I came along, and . . . and what?" Hannah started, wishing she sounded more benevolent, less accusatory. "I wasn't enough?"

Her father frowned. "You came along and she—and I guess a part of me as well—became afraid. That you'd leave us . . . too."

Hannah pulled a chair from the table, and only then noticed that her hands were shaking.

"I know your mom and I haven't always been there for you, especially these last few years. We thought having more kids would help us forget, move past it somehow. And it did. I thought it did. Kerry came along and your mother was distracted with having another baby around the house. You were clearly pulling away, and Kerry became her little doll. For a while, it seemed to work. I'm not saying it's right, Hannah. But how can anyone forget losing a child?"

How can anyone forget the child that lived? Hannah dug her nails into her upper arms, hesitating. "Did *you* . . . ever forget?"

"No," he said softly, staring into his hands again and drawing small circles on his palm.

The motor in the refrigerator kicked on, and Hannah remembered her rumbling stomach. "Maybe you should stop trying." She let her words fill the room above the hum. She re-crossed her arms over her chest and held on to her shoulders.

"You've always been so smart . . . have I told you that?" he said, watching her now.

"You just did."

CHAPTER 36

———

THE NEXT MORNING, HANNAH MADE HER WAY TO THE BUS
stop feeling strangely subdued. Her dad had actually been
pretty decent and offered to get her excused from school the
rest of the week, but she'd declined. She didn't want to hang
around the house; the dead air was too depressing, and she
could still see her mom's and Kerry's bodies lying motionless
everywhere she looked.

"Hannah, I know you were the one who found them . . .
getting the ambulance here in time . . ." her dad had said before heading up to bed. She knew it was the closest she'd get
to a thank-you. So she took it.

The afternoon when Hannah found them, all of the
neighbors, ones she hadn't seen in years, were *miraculously* out
walking their dog or getting their mail in time to watch her
mother being carried out on a stretcher, followed by her little
sister. The buzz on the street heightened when Kerry's heart
got restarted just before the ambulance doors closed. Hannah
glared at the parade of downturned mouths and shaking
heads. *Screw 'em*, she thought and walked back into the
house.

It would be another week or two before Hannah could

see her mom or sister again, something about their bodies needing to go through stages of withdrawal. The doctors used words with her dad like "possible seizures," "chance of brain damage," and "near death." *Please God, don't let my mother and sister die.*

Her father told the hospital medical staff and social worker that he'd mistaken her mother's pill bottle for Kerry's vitamins, that he'd given her the pills by accident . . . with his poor eyesight and all. *Different story, different day,* Hannah thought. But it had been enough to keep Child Protective Services from taking her baby sister away.

The real truth Hannah knew in her heart was that her mother had gone from doctor to doctor, just about anyone she could charm, to write her—or Hannah—prescriptions. *To. Just. Not. Feel. Anything.* Hannah guessed that her mom hadn't banked on the inevitable—craving her little helper to the point of obsession and at her youngest daughter's expense. To cover her tracks, her mom had even filled her scripts at a number of pharmacies outside of town, always with little Kerry and Droge bear in tow.

Just six years old. Hannah's guilt consumed her when it came to Kerry. She should have been watching out for her. What the hell had happened to her family? She still couldn't believe that there had been another baby. The thought of having an older sibling sent her mind awhirl. If he had lived, maybe she wouldn't have been born at all. Or maybe they would have grown up together, been best friends. He would have shown her the ropes. No bully would have ever touched her with a big brother at her side. Even now, he would be protecting her. Hannah sighed at all the what-ifs.

The December wind blasted her face as she neared the top of the street, causing her eyes to tear. She pulled her hair from her mouth with a new thought. Maybe her brother hadn't survived because he wasn't meant to be born to save her, protect her from all the teenage crap and people like Deacon. Perhaps she had to learn to go it alone.

You are better than them. Smarter. Braver. Stop getting in your own way. Believe in yourself. You, Hannah Zandana, can be and do anything. They're afraid of you. Now act like it. Go.

———

Taylor stood alone at the bus stop in another one of her varsity football jackets. She seemed preoccupied, pacing back and forth with her arms folded over her chest. *What a drama queen*, Hannah thought. But then again, she could just be cold.

She glanced around. Where were the other girls? She smiled at the idea that the coven had finally imploded on itself. Still, Taylor was acting strangely. She drew closer, and when she spotted the embroidered name on her letterman jacket, she did a double take.

"You're dating Toby now?" Hannah stopped in her tracks, her outburst practically knocking the girl over.

"Yeah, why do you care?" Taylor replied, her voice sounding more damsel-in-distress than tough-girl. Hannah almost felt sorry for her.

"He's sooo not your type."

"Shut up, like you would know. Heard Deacon dumped you, *finally.*"

Hannah took a step forward, looking Taylor squarely in the eye. "Maybe you shouldn't believe everything you hear."

She stomped onto the bus and slid into her usual seat next to Peter.

"You doing all right?" he asked in a low voice after Taylor had made her way past their seat.

His steady kindness brought tears to Hannah's eyes. She quickly blinked them away before they had a chance to drop. She knew he was alluding to the ambulance at her house. By now the whole school must be abuzz. It was only a matter of time until everyone started drawing their conclusions about what happened, if they hadn't already.

"Not really," she said, keeping her eyes locked on the back of the bus driver's greasy, flake-filled head.

"Looks like you defrosted from the other day," he said with a small smile.

"Thanks, Peter." *For not asking me to explain.*

He stayed close to her when they got off the bus, holding the door for her as she walked underneath his arm and escorting her to her locker. His presence was comforting. Even after he left her side, with a small knowing nod, she felt safer knowing he wasn't far away.

Hannah sighed, looking at the mountain of books in her locker. She felt dazed for a moment, trying to figure what she needed for her next few classes. But the quiet moment didn't last; suddenly, Gillian and Leeza descended on her like vultures.

"So, skank, what's the *deal* with your mom and sister?" Gillian shouted into the hallway, screwing up her face like she'd just smelled rotten eggs. Hannah wasn't about to give her the satisfaction, though her insides were already twisting. She pursed her lips and turned back to close her locker.

Gillian grabbed her shoulder and spun her around, setting Leeza off into a gale of nervous laugher and making her Queen of Hearts "Elect Me!" button jiggle on her boobs.

"Don't fricking touch me!" Hannah glared at Gillian—the same little witch who'd never played nice in the sandbox, who'd always tormented people just for kicks. Feeling the blood rise in her face, she clenched her right hand, shaking more with fear than hatred. But then Toby's Neanderthal presence came out of nowhere, taking up space next to Gillian, and Hannah felt her anger transforming into tears.

Then Mrs. Myers's face popped into her head.

"I'm not afraid of you, Gillian. Take your *perverted* pals and go *F* yourselves!"

Stunned, Toby and Leeza looked to Gillian for what to do next, neither of them noticing the color draining from the redhead's face.

Before they could recover, Hannah bolted away, praying they wouldn't come after her.

CHAPTER 37

december 1989

THE BLOOD BEHIND HIS EYES SEIZED HIS TEMPLES WITH A truth he could no longer resist. He'd made a business out of populating the town with addicts, and now, somehow, he'd become one himself. He had to get her back. If only he could kiss her again and be saved from this torture.

He parked his car behind a white van a half block from her house. The swirling December wind wound around his car and rattled its windows and floorboards. He exhaled the cold air through his nose in two white puffs.

Something in his chest was gnawing him over not seeing her. Nearly two weeks without her and he knew he was in love with her and longed to get her back—back into the fold of his arms, back where she belonged.

Deacon didn't know how he'd gotten here, but he knew the longer he was without her, the more it hurt. Nothing mattered anymore. He couldn't sleep, just walked around at night thinking about her. He'd cut up the pictures of her as soon as she had left that day. He loathed his fucking horny self for keeping them.

Finally, Hannah's father's car came down the street from the other direction and pulled into the driveway. Deacon's lips parted, drinking in every inch of her. Her curly hair was wild in the wind as she pulled her down jacket around her. She was wearing his favorite jeans, the ones with the rip in the knee, and a pair of boots he hadn't seen before. If only he could talk to her. But she disappeared too quickly into the house.

Jade had found out from her cousin at the hospital where they had taken Hannah's mother and sister the week earlier. He'd thought about trying to see her there, but decided to wait. Deacon knew a few junkies hooked on Valium, but he'd never come across someone's mom or a little kid getting caught up in it. He wished he'd known sooner about the overdoses, helped her through somehow. Mostly, he wished he could still climb through her window and hold her like that time before.

Deacon's daydream came to a halt at the sight of the green Chevy two-door coming down the street. His gaze hardened, recognizing its driver; the same guy who liked to stare him down when he'd meet Hannah's bus in the morning.

"Fuck you if you think you're getting anywhere with her," Deacon spat at the dashboard. He watched Peter walk up to ring the doorbell with a thick book resting in his hand. Deacon flinched seeing the smile she gave him when she opened the door. The exchange was brief, but Deacon already had his hand on the door handle; he'd never been more ready to pummel somebody. But Jack's voice came into his head: *Never let them see you sweat, Little D.* He stopped himself and released a long sigh. He crossed his arms over the steering wheel, feeling extraordinarily tired.

"Just how do I get you back?" he whispered, his frosty breath floating away.

CHAPTER 38

"So how are you holding up?" Mrs. Myers asked her after class. Hannah immediately looked around to see if anyone could hear them, but thankfully the classroom had emptied.

"Okay . . . I guess." Hannah shrugged.

"If the rumors are true, you've been through a lot lately."

Hannah's face dropped. *Really, you too, Mrs. Myers?*

"Sorry, I should rephrase that," her teacher said hastily, seeming to realize her mistake. "I heard about your mom and sister, that had to be scary for you."

Hannah nodded somberly. "Thanks." She spun around toward the door.

"Hannah, if you ever . . ."

She glanced back and was struck by the softness in her teacher's eyes. She took a deep breath. "I appreciate you looking out. Really, you've been great."

"The rest is up to you?"

"The rest is up to me." Hannah nodded and grinned.

"Go."

Hannah headed to her locker, feeling slightly lighter but still spent as she did her best to ignore the occasional looks from her classmates. *None of this matters anymore*, she told herself, holding her head up and soldiering on like nothing could stop her.

"Hannah Zandana!" It was the same loudmouth boy who'd been teasing her since freshman year. This time, he was standing with a couple of other senior boys near the water fountain. She turned back and caught them snickering at her and snapping their gum. Hannah clenched her teeth and charged right up to ringleader, the tiny hairs on her neck all standing at attention.

"Dude, what's your problem?" she challenged him. "You're being annoying."

The loudmouth kid's jaw fell to the floor like he'd just been asked a complicated algebra problem he couldn't answer. He turned back to his friends, but they each looked the other way, leaving him hanging. Even the hallway quieted, but Hannah's stare down didn't falter.

After a moment, the boy shrugged. "Ahh, I'm just kidding," he said sheepishly. "Didn't mean anything—"

Hannah turned on her heel, swinging her hair behind her. She walked away without hearing a peep from anyone.

When she got to her locker, she swung open the door and began surveying its contents.

"Friday, Friday . . . what do I need . . . math . . . social studies?" she murmured to herself, filling up her book bag for the long winter break. Out of nowhere, one of her thick textbooks jumped off the top metal shelf, its sharp corner hitting her on the head. She rubbed the offended area a few times, and that's when she saw it: a folded white piece of spiral loose-leaf near her shoe. She didn't recognize the handwriting, but then again she wasn't accustomed to getting notes from anyone.

Whatever you do, don't go to Gossamer Park with Toby, Gillian, or even Jade. It's a trap. D

———

Hannah mulled over the note on the bus ride home. An uneasiness spread through her belly, but she wasn't sure if she should be worried or not. What did it mean, exactly? She glanced at the empty seats around her. The bus was unusually quiet for the day before winter break. The coven, too, was absent. Maybe everyone had taken off early for some Florida sunshine, or to Vail to ski. *Must be nice.*

Stepping off at her corner, she immediately recognized the tan-skinned brunette from the park. She was leaning out of a blue BMW, smiling and waving at her. The driver, a preppy blond-haired guy, looked bored to bits as his passenger yelled to her, "Hannah! Hey . . . Deacon wanted me to give you a message."

"I think I already got it," Hannah said, eyeing her cautiously. The sweet smell of pot wafted from the car, reminding her of the Halloween party.

"He wants you to meet him in the park tonight," she said, flashing Hannah one of her gleaming smiles like they were friends. Jade turned to the boy in the car, lowering her voice so Hannah couldn't hear, then turned back with another smile. "Gill said meet at 8:00 p.m., I—I meant Deacon, 8:00 p.m., okay?"

Jade's misstep reminded Hannah of Deacon's account of

her getting flustered by the undercover cop coming back from the city.

"So which is it, Deacon or Gillian who wants to meet with me?" Hannah's eyes narrowed, knowing without a doubt that she'd be calling Deacon's beeper as soon as she got home. She started to walk away.

"Wait! Hannah . . . he's doing this for you," Jade called out, slamming her hand against the car door.

"What are you talking about?"

"Deacon said he messed up and needed to do something."

"He said that?" Hannah wanted to believe her but questioned Jade's motive and her loyalty to Deacon, not to mention her relationship with that redheaded terror. The girl really did play both sides.

"Gillian's really wiggin' out, I've never seen her like this . . . she said some stuff to Toby that got him trippin'. You need to book it to the park tonight, Toby is going to do something . . . and it's bad."

Hannah dialed Deacon's home number and beeper for over an hour, but there was no response or returned call. She raided the scant offerings in the fridge and tried to watch TV, all the while convincing herself she was better off staying home. It was definitely safer than showing up in that dark park alone, she reasoned. There was the note, though. But did Deacon really write it? Or did someone else . . . Gillian? No, that didn't make much sense. She felt queasy, and the knot in her stomach was only expanding. She reached for the phone.

"Peter . . . Hi, I need a favor. Can you come get me? Yes . . . now . . . something's going down."

CHAPTER 39

———

"STOP THE CAR! STOP THE CAR!" HANNAH JUMPED OUT before Peter brought it to a stop. Leaving him behind, she raced to the same spot in Gossamer Park where she and Deacon had first made out under the big towering oak trees. She couldn't hear their voices but she saw them in the distance, the breath escaping from their lips looking like white daggers.

It's a trap Deacon's words echoed in her head. She needed to stay out of the light of the street lamps and move slowly and carefully; she couldn't afford to fall or make noise. When she was most of the way there, she crouched low to the ground behind some large bushes for a moment or two, catching her breath and blowing on her hands to warm them. Then she moved closer.

Hannah could hear them now as she ventured back out. She hid behind a huge oak tree where she was close enough to see what was happening. Her breath cut off sharply at the sight of Deacon and Toby circling one another like sharks on the other side of its massive trunk. The street lamps illuminated their faces, but Deacon kept walking in and out of the shadows, making it hard to read his face. From where Hannah stood, they looked like they'd come alone.

Toby stopped circling and put up his hands. "I'm not here

for you bro, where's your girlfriend? Oh that's right, you guys broke up. Pretty lame, dude, that sophomore girl breaking it off first."

"You're not going to touch her. Gillian's plan is off."

"She must have done something to really piss off our Gilly girl. She's out for blood, bro." He reached into his pocket, but came out empty-handed.

"So you're working for Gillian now?" Deacon sneered.

"Nah, we have an understanding, that's all." Toby hesitated, watching Deacon's face. "She knows what I want . . . I know what she wants."

"And what is that, exactly?" Deacon challenged, acting like he was already over the conversation. Hannah remembered him saying that Toby was about as threatening as a Cub Scout and not half as smart.

"Gillian wants me to scare the crap out of Hannah to keep her from telling everyone whatever she knows."

Deacon laughed smugly. "Bet you don't even know what that is—totally clueless!"

Toby shrugged, his eyes steady on Deacon.

"And the money for the abortion?" Deacon asked bluntly, his patience evidently waning.

"I was never going to let her kill it—c'mon, you've got to believe me. I just wanted the money. Yeah, I said it. I wanted to see if you'd do one right by me." Toby stomped the ground. "Guess what, you couldn't even do that, bro!"

"Don't call me that! I'm NOT your fucking brother," Deacon screamed.

A shiver curled around Hannah's ears. She'd never seen him like this.

Toby began to pace. "What the fuck! Why do you mess with me when you know the truth?"

Deacon leaned back and let out a low cackle, shaking his head.

"It's bullshit, D, and you know it. That's why Kingsley tried to pay my mom off . . . sent me to that boarding school, same one old Pierre sent you. Remember, dude, not so long ago? But it's all about appearances, isn't it? Keeping me a secret to protect his *precious* election."

"More like his *precious son!*" Deacon shouted without meeting Toby's eyes, his face now visibly upset.

"What did you say?"

"You heard me, you bastard! Your mom's just some *whore* my dad screwed on the side . . . and out came her white-trash *bastard* child! And lookie here, history repeats itself: you get a girl pregnant. A bastard having a bastard!"

"Stop it, stop saying that!" Toby rushed Deacon and threw him off his feet like he was sacking a quarterback. He landed a few punches to Deacon's head.

Hannah could barely stop herself from running out from behind the tree and throwing herself at Toby; she didn't know how much she could take. Somehow, she had to help Deacon.

Then Deacon shoved Toby away forcefully, putting some distance between them.

Toby rose, staggering at first, and readied himself to go again. He reached inside his jacket.

"Fucking bastard!" Deacon snarled, getting up slowly and wiping the blood from his forehead. "Just a matter of time until you cry and run off like last time—"

He stopped short at the sight of the shiny metal now shaking in Toby's hands. Hannah let out a gasp.

Straightening his arm, Toby began to sob, wiping the snot from his upper lip.

"Stop it! Stop fucking saying that!" he cried, stumbling backward and blinking furiously.

Deacon smiled sweetly, mocking him. Then he circled Toby, with his arms outstretched like he was some demigod. "What are *you* going to do about it?" His words came out dark and guttural, like he was possessed. "You think my father's all that great? You're smoking something. You can have the asshole, you fucking prick. Merry Fucking Christmas to you. You think he was ever there for *me?* Nine fucking years he let that woman leave me with that asshole! *Nine.* What makes you think you're any different? My father *used me* to complete his perfect family picture. That's right. I'm an accessory. He fucking never wanted me. Fuck, he barely talks to me. HE IGNORES ME!"

Deacon flinched and hid his face from Toby. His shoulders fell and his pace quickened. He flexed his hands a couple of times, then lunged toward Toby.

A shot sounded.

"No!" Hannah cried as Deacon faded to the ground.

"Fuck you, fuck you!" Toby screamed, tears falling down his face. He didn't even look in Hannah's direction. "All I ever wanted was to be your brother . . . for our dad to claim I was a Giroux too. *A goddamn Giroux.* He ruined my mom's life. And you've ruined mine. Why?" He cried harder. "Fucking why? I just wanted you to be my brother, have a family . . . LOOK WHAT YOU MADE ME DO!"

Toby doubled over with a low, grating groan that didn't sound human. He smacked his head repeatedly and fell to his knees. Then he pushed the tip of the gun into his temple.

Oh my god. Hannah tasted the sourness of whatever she'd eaten coming up her throat before her body heaved over. As she stumbled out from behind the tree, a branch snapped and the gun swerved off Toby's head. She took off toward Deacon, but Toby intercepted her and grabbed her by the waist.

"Let me go!" she pleaded. *Think fast, think fast.*

"No one can know," he said darkly pointing the weapon at her chest.

"What? Stop this," Hannah cried, unable to get enough air in her lungs. She swallowed hard, coughing. "Your father . . . Toby, your father would be so *proud* of you. You did him a favor. Got rid of the bad son and now the good son can join the family. Isn't that what you always wanted—to be his precious son, take your rightful place?"

"How would you know anything about it?" said Toby, eyeing her suspiciously.

"Deacon told me. He's been such a disappointment to your dad, walking around like some Goth, the high school drug dealer. Nothing but a low-life."

Toby shook his head. "Bullshit! I saw the way Kingsley looked at him."

"No, Toby, it was *you*. You're the son he always wanted. Look at you, the smart varsity football player, perfect in every way. Handsome too, like your dad." Hannah prayed that she hadn't overplayed it.

Toby looked around like he didn't know where he was. He dropped the gun to his side and staggered backward, wincing and gripping the side of his head. All at once, his rigid stance caved, his knees sank again into the frozen ground. Just then, Peter sprang from the shadows and jumped on Toby's back. The larger boy's head smacked the ground.

Hannah seized her chance; she hurled herself toward Deacon. His body was twisted strangely, and she immediately saw her own mother sprawled on the kitchen floor. "God, please not again," she prayed aloud. "Please, God, help me!" She rolled Deacon onto his back and that's when she saw it, blood spreading through his shirt on the right side of his chest. She pulled off her pom-pom hat and applied pressure. But the blood was coming out too fast. "No, no, no! You can't die. Please, Deacon, hold on. We'll get you some help. Please, please don't die!"

CHAPTER 40

DEACON STIRRED AT THE SOUND OF HER VOICE. HIS EYES were slits as he tried to talk through the warm liquid pooling in his mouth. He managed a small smile for her. "Yum, nothing like the taste of metal."

"Please, don't leave me!" Hannah cried, searching around them, calling out to the darkness, "Help us! He's been shot. Somebody help!"

"Hannah." Deacon's voice was weak. "Should never have let you leave."

"Please God, save him, please, oh God," she cried.

"Hannah, shhhh," Deacon whispered, but she wasn't listening. He wished he could hold her and for the pain to stop. Hannah knew everything now—all of his secrets—and she'd never been more beautiful.

"*Sirens!* They're coming, Deacon, they're coming! I hear them. Stay with me. Just stay with me. Please . . . baby."

Hannah didn't know how long she'd been holding Deacon's chest before her legs grew numb underneath her. At some point he stopped responding to her, his face peaceful. It reminded her of their first time together, when she engraved him into her memory. She felt she was going crazy.

Wait, his chest is still rising, isn't it? Her first two fingers flew to the side of his neck, then to the inside of his wrist, and back again. Nothing.

"He's still alive, I know he is," she cried as strong hands lifted her to her feet. "See his breath . . . I still see it . . . please believe me . . . he's not—"

"Come on, Hannah, it's time to go home." Hannah crumbled into his arms. He caught her before she fell.

Hannah didn't remember her dad bringing her to her feet or driving her home. She woke up several times screaming that night, once as she was yelling at Toby not to shoot, watching the blood pool from Deacon's body, and then as the tribe of cops yelled at her about the gun. "*Where's the frigging gun?*" they shouted again and again. "Peter threw it into the lake," she told them. "He saved us."

That was what had happened, wasn't it?

That same night, she dreamt of being at Deacon's funeral. She was standing in the back among the curious crowd, none of them friends or acquaintances of the boy she'd lost. But she wasn't surprised by that. Like her, he didn't have many friends.

The uneven staccato of Mrs. Giroux's heels against the marble floor hushed the onlookers when Kingsley and Babette strode through the side door behind the officiating priest, avoiding the church's lengthy center aisle and throng of rubberneckers. Kingsley's hands hung in tight fists, his face was reddened, his chapped lips were the color of chalk. Babette's powdered complexion and red-painted mouth wobbled atop a self-conscious stride, like she'd forgotten how to walk. Both followed the man in the robe closely, two ghostlike bodies drained of color and ravaged by grief. Or so it appeared. Hannah could almost feel sorry for them, but didn't.

The pair teetered oddly near the altar by Deacon's coffin, leaving an uncomfortable gap between them. The priest was a couple of minutes into his delivery when Babette collapsed. The sound of her head crashing into the marble floor reverberated through the cathedral like a tuning fork. Whispers escalated, and Hannah could sense the congregation turning on Kingsley. All around her, angry eyes ripped through the back of Deacon's father's head, demanding that he do something. But he just stood there until the priest tapped the side of his arm. Only then did Kingsley react—first pulling back in shock then shaking like he was a lost boy in a supermarket. His long legs folded underneath him at the same time his manicured fingers reached for his wife's body. She lay still on the ground, her winter-white houndstooth suit soaking up the blood from the floor.

Hannah woke with a start. Her cheeks were wet and her chest hurt like hell. She blinked a few times as she looked around her bedroom, putting a hand to her heart to regain her breath. In her stillness, the dream slowly dissolved, but the nightmare remained. *He's not dead; he's not dead. Please . . .*

CHAPTER 41

THERE WASN'T GOING TO BE A PUBLIC FUNERAL, ACCORDING to the five o'clock Action 7 News lady, a spunky, doe-eyed reporter who stood under Hannah and Deacon's towering oaks in the park wearing a full-length down coat with a matching knit hat and mittens, gripping her microphone like a beauty contestant.

Hannah glared at the TV. *Bitch, you don't know a thing about it.* For a moment, she pretended that Toby was the one who had died and not Deacon. The thought of it gave her a dizzy, floating feeling; loosening the grip of numbness she'd felt since she heard the gun go off that night. But Miss Reporter Girl set her straight too quickly for it to last.

"As Deacon Giroux's classmates mourn his tragic death just days before Christmas, sadly one local prominent family is reeling over the loss of its precious son . . . and at the hand of his own brother. This is Shawna James from Action 7 News. Back to you, Bob."

Hannah moped around the house the next few days, blowing off showering and meals and spending her time wandering in and out of rooms or sitting and staring at some soap opera or game show on TV with the volume turned off.

She slept very little, and dreaded the evenings the most—that was when the loneliness and pain of losing Deacon would bubble to the surface and send her screaming into her pillow until she'd cried so much she could do nothing else but finally surrender to sleep.

One night, the sound of Deacon tapping urgently on her window stirred her from a deep slumber. Her body snapped straight up in bed. She knew he'd come back for her *because he loved her.* She didn't care who heard them; she'd go anywhere with him. She'd leave tonight and get away from the pain of living in this house. The lump in her chest filled with air and buoyed her up; she could breathe again, every cell was resuscitated and ushered back to life. She sprang to her feet and craned her neck to look down over the windowsill and catch him standing below her. But no one was there.

Her father arrived home after work on Christmas Eve with a bag of drugstore gifts from the Pathmark near their house for her to wrap: perfume and a quilted toiletry bag for her mother, a couple of knock-off Care Bears for Kerry, a curling iron and makeup from the bargain bin for her, and a new ice scraper for the car. *Merry Fucking Christmas,* she could hear Deacon saying. God, she missed him.

Hannah and her father rode in silence Christmas morning to spend some time with her mother and sister at the rehabilitation facility. They hadn't spoken much since that awful night in the park, outside of discussing what groceries were needed for the house and where the wrapping paper was located. Neither of them had the energy to pull the Christmas decorations from the attic. Hannah didn't feel like talking and wasn't about to share with her father what she was going through—not like he asked her anyway. Keeping the pain of losing Deacon inside somehow kept him alive for her. And that was all she had left.

"Hannah?" Her father looked at her impatiently.

"What? Sorry."

"I said . . . regarding that kid who got shot, maybe next time you'll select better friends."

Hannah's jaw clenched, and every expletive she knew ran through her head. She couldn't look at him. He didn't deserve it. "I don't have any friends," she croaked, glaring out her window.

"The boy . . . the one who died?"

"He's . . ." Hannah closed her eyes. "He . . . was nobody," she whispered into her shoulder.

The rehab facility, unlike their bleak, dirty house, was decorated for practically every December holiday, from Christmas and Chanukah, to New Year's. The cheesy ornaments, tinsel, and plastic poinsettias around the nurses' station and along the usually stark walls made the place especially depressing when set against its somber crew of patients, whose eyes told her that they'd rather be anywhere but there. Hannah passed a cardboard cutout of a Yule log at the entrance to her mother's room. Kerry was in a chair beside her mother, who was sitting up in bed, and they were playing Candy Land on the overbed table. Both of them glanced up when she and her father entered.

Her mom looked small compared to her hospital bed. Her face was different, too—puffier, Hannah thought. The two of them had been there a little over two weeks, with Kerry being treated upstairs in the children's ward. With the drugs drained from her system, her mother's face appeared smoother and less creased around the eyes and mouth. Hannah kept staring at this new, softer version before her. Kerry, too, had gained some weight and no longer resembled a mini skeleton.

"Kerry, let's go see if we can find Santa himself wandering the hallways," her dad said, lifting his daughter into his arms. Kerry smiled up at him and nestled her head into his neck like she was a baby as he carried her out the door.

A little panic rose in Hannah's chest with the two of them gone. Should she sit or stand, or go over and hug her mother? *What does one do when visiting half the family in rehab?*

A couple of nurses rushed by the doorway and a man down the hall began yelling to one of them. Hannah closed the door and leaned against the wall with her hands behind her back. She watched her mother, who gathered the game pieces in her hand, then collected the cards, carefully facing them in the same direction before placing the stack on top of the game board and closing the box. When she finished, she folded her hands in her lap and looked up at Hannah expectantly.

What immediately struck Hannah was how still she was. Gone was the restlessness and jittery energy, not to mention the flat, empty eyes. The woman in front of her was poised and alert.

"It's okay . . . I won't break," her mom said carefully with a faint smile that quickly fell into a frown. "Merry Christmas."

"Merry Christmas."

"This isn't easy, is it?"

Hannah shook her head and her throat tightened.

"I've been dishonest with you . . . with everyone. As we're told to say at the start of every therapy session, 'My name is Donna and I'm an addict.'" She wiped her eyes like she was crying, but she wasn't. "A low-life, middle-aged addict . . . how pathetic is that," she said softly, her lips twisting along with the bedsheet that was threaded through her fingers. "Do you know what the worst part is? I'm a horrid mother. Look at what I did to Kerry."

And me, Hannah thought.

"I was so afraid I'd be found out. It took over my life. I know I don't deserve anyone's forgiveness . . ."

Hannah kept staring at her mother. *Who is this woman?* Valium, Vicodin, wine, and whatever else she'd been taking to numb herself had altered her personality so much that Hannah was now in the presence of a stranger—one who could turn on her in a heartbeat, the voice in her head warned.

"Your dad told you about the baby . . . Michael."

Hannah nodded slowly, stunned to hear her say his name.

"The doctors say his death stirred up some past issues for me," she said, knotting her fingers together, twisting them like roots gnarled in the ground. Her neck was getting blotchy and her words raspy, like she couldn't get enough air.

"You okay, Mom? Do you need some water?"

She shook her head. "I used to wake up with these panic attacks, thinking I was smothering your brother in the bed. Your father would find me digging through the sheets, looking for the baby. My anxiety got so bad, he took me to the doctor. That's when it all started."

A round, plump nurse in a royal blue uniform blouse with a Christmas tree pin at the collar suddenly moved through the door, whistling a Christmas tune through her teeth. She crossed the room to the bathroom as they both waited. Hannah heard the woman dumping something in the toilet and flushing it. She then reappeared at her mother's bedside and lifted the water pitcher to check its contents. Holding the carafe on her hip, the nurse glanced over at Hannah leaning against the wall but didn't say anything. Her mother gave the woman a knowing smile that reached her eyes like they were old friends. Hannah felt like she was witnessing a private joke.

"I'm her daughter," Hannah said, clearing her throat and stepping forward just in case she wanted to shake her hand.

"I didn't know you had another daughter, Miss Donna. She live with you?"

Hannah's mother closed her eyes and nodded.

Gee, thanks Mom.

"Well, you're looking better today. Need anything?"

Her mother shook her head slowly, producing an angelic doe-eyed expression that made Hannah want to laugh out loud. *Who is* she *kidding?*

The nurse patted Hannah's mother's hand before she left. Hannah remained invisible, holding up the wall.

Her mother waited then cleared her throat again. "Hannah, listen—the way your dad is hard on you . . . my father was the same way." Her voice trailed off, and she turned toward the lone window in the room. Hannah followed her eyes, feeling like they were on the verge of a breakthrough; finally her mother would share her secrets and Hannah could tell her all about Deacon. "He just wants you to grow into a nice young lady—"

"And the names he calls me . . . 'harlot' . . . 'whore' . . . those are supposed to help?"

"Oh, Hannah . . . you bring that on yourself."

CHAPTER 42

"THERE'S A GIRL OUTSIDE, PROBABLY LOITERING AND UP to no good. I don't like it. It's like she's casing the place to rob us or something," her father announced from his favorite recliner, hitting his hand with a section of the newspaper that he'd rolled into a tight tube. Hannah followed her father's gaze out the front window. A girl was smoking out there, her ripped jean bottom perched prettily on the curb. *Jade*. She flicked her cigarette to the street when she saw Hannah.

"Never mind. She's here for me." She took a deep breath before opening the front door.

"He was my friend, too," Jade said with an edge in her voice when she reached the porch.

Hannah didn't answer and wasn't sure if she should let her inside.

"Um, can we talk?"

Hannah shrugged and led her into the kitchen. She could hear her dad ascending the stairs to his room. She motioned to one of the chairs, but Jade stood. They both did, sharing the uncomfortable proximity. Hannah notice that she looked struck by the burnt orange starburst clock in the kitchen, like she'd never known anything so ugly could ever exist.

"So . . ."

"I'm so sorry . . . I didn't think . . . it all went way too far
. . . so fast. I should have stopped her, stopped Toby . . ."

Hannah's brows knitted together at the girl's chattering
confession, she felt dizzy and disoriented. Deacon had been
gone a little over two weeks and this was the first time she'd
been forced to talk about him. She slid into one of the chairs.
Jade plopped down in the one next to her. Then she suddenly
bolted up and began pacing, her jumpy expression fluctuating
between Hannah's face and the linoleum while she nervously
picked at the seared skin on one of her fingers. Gone were
her once-glowing green eyes and honey-colored skin; they'd
been replaced by a haunting, gaunt face with a greenish pal-
lor. She had nasty burn marks on her upper lip, too. She
looked run over.

Jade stopped and leaned her face uncomfortably close to
Hannah's. "I know what I do with Gillian *disgusts* you—"

Hannah's head jerked back. "You don't disgust me, Jade. I
don't think about it. You have every right to be with her. I
would never have exposed you and Gillian. No matter how
much I loathe her, I would not have done that."

Jade stilled. A look of surprise combined with relief tran-
spired on her face. "Oh my God, oh my God," she said, col-
lapsing back into the chair, her hands running through her
hair. "He's really dead isn't he? I can't fucking deal with this . . ."

"Your girlfriend did this and I have no way to prove it.
You're all protecting her."

"I know, *I know* . . ."

"Why . . . what the *hell?*"

"Gill is terrified of anyone discovering . . . you know . . .
us. She's also pissed at me, at Deacon, for getting involved in

dealing . . . using, too. You know, just sometimes," she said, checking Hannah's face. "I don't know . . . she just wigged out. Then Toby came along and she realized they shared a common enemy—"

"But I heard them talking just before it happened. Toby wanted Deacon in his life . . . wanted to be a Giroux," Hannah said.

"He still does, I'm sure."

"What did you say?"

Jade nervously coughed. "He didn't go to the park to kill Deacon."

Hannah blinked several times. "You told me to go to Gossamer for Deacon, when all along, you know it was *me* they were after." Hannah slammed her hand down on the table and pushed herself up from her chair.

Jade grabbed Hannah's hand. "No one was supposed to die that night . . . I swear."

"*Toby*—"

"Fucked up . . . The cops believe it to be accidental . . . an argument between two brothers . . . I'm so sorry . . . God, I wish I could take it all back."

Jade's tears made Hannah realize that she, herself, didn't have any left to shed. Hannah knew she'd been duped, lied to, and played for a fool—and for what? Power. Love. Acceptance? All to fix her sad, pathetic life? *Yep, it was what you wanted*, the voice inside her head bellowed.

"Deacon really loved you, Hannah."

Hannah took a long, deep breath, and the truth revealed itself to her in that moment. "He loved the power—and the drugs—more."

CHAPTER 43

THAT NIGHT, HANNAH SPOTTED HER FATHER'S ROLLED newspaper from earlier in the day stuck inside the kitchen trash. She pulled it out slowly, flicking off a slimy piece of onion. Her mouth grew dry even before she unrolled it, but still she needed to see it.

Just the headline made Hannah crumple it up, her head falling back into her shoulders. She closed her eyes, released a silent cry, and pulled her cardigan around herself. Then she sank down into one of the kitchen chairs and smoothed the pages out again.

GOSSAMER PARK SHOOTING

Hannah's and Peter's names didn't appear in the story, just Deacon's and Toby's, along with those of their parents. It was like Hannah had never existed. The murder weapon retrieved from the lake had come from Kingsley's private gun collection. Thinking of his father, Hannah thought, *God, that has to hurt.* There was no mention of the charges filed against Toby. Her eyes skimmed the rest until she saw them side-by-side, their senior yearbook pictures taken over the summer just five months earlier, both suntanned and seemingly happy: two brothers born months apart, one a jock, the other a drug dealer, both abandoned, both lost.

You could see the family resemblance in their eyes, the same brown hue translated differently on each of their faces. Definitely brothers. *How did I miss that?* Hannah wondered. She traced Deacon's picture with her finger, stopping on his lips. For a minute she was right back there, gazing into that extraordinary face, reliving all of their sensual kisses and the way electricity would fire through her body, down to her toes. But he'd become so much more to her during their short time together; they'd shared a connection no one could possibly understand. Two outsiders from crappy homes with parents who didn't understand or bother to know them.

She'd been his, once, and she'd give anything to have him back. Hannah dug the bottom edge of her palms into her eyes, thinking if she just pressed hard enough, somehow it wouldn't hurt so much.

Finally, she opened her eyes again and pushed the paper aside, but not before her eye caught the sidebar to the right: LT. GOVERNOR ELECT KINGSLEY GIROUX STEPS DOWN. Hannah's body folded over the table, her throbbing, tired head resting like dead weight on her forearms; suddenly, it was all too heavy to hold up.

———

Hannah fell further into hopelessness after that, sleeping mostly during the day and waking up for long stretches at night—always after a dream about Deacon. Unable to fall back to sleep, she'd sit on top of her bed, holding her knees to her chest, and listen to the world outside her window—the occasional car whizzing down the street with the radio blasting, trees being pushed around by the wind, and the nightly feral cat brawl—still pretending that he was coming for her.

Trays of food began to show up on her dresser as she lost track of time altogether. The sound of the doorbell would remind her when it was daytime again. Once she heard Peter trying to make conversation with her dad. He left her a book to read.

One afternoon, she awoke to someone sitting near the foot of her bed. She opened her eyes, thinking her mother had come home.

"I just wanted to see how you were doing. I'm sorry for what happened." On cue, Taylor began to cry like one of those soap opera actresses Hannah had been watching recently. "If I'd known what Toby was going to do, I would have stopped him, told somebody. Guess I didn't know him at all."

Hannah sat up. The girl pressed her lips together, eyeing Hannah's bedhead, and waited for Hannah to respond. She seemed genuinely sad as she cried, but there was something irritating about her movements. It was the way she held her stomach, consciously rubbing it to get Hannah's attention.

"Taylor?"

"Yeah."

"You really are pregnant, aren't you?"

"Afraid so. Six months," she said, perking up.

"Oh my God, what are you going to do?"

"What is there to do? Have it. Give it up for adoption. Pretend it never happened. My mother can't even look at me."

"How long were you with Toby?"

"Oh, it's not Toby's. Some guy I met eons ago. Summer fling, you know? I just said that it was Toby's. I had no idea he'd go ape-shit and threaten Deacon for the abortion money." She sniffed. "From what I heard, Mr. Giroux didn't even know that Toby had changed schools. He was still paying his mother for that private boys school up north," she said, suddenly quite dry-eyed and matter-of-fact.

"Why did you let Toby think it was his?" Hannah asked, feeling the blood course up her neck and into her temples.

Taylor looked at Hannah like she'd just said something stupid. "Toby fell so hard for me, so quickly and everything, that I knew he'd do anything I asked . . . "

Hannah closed her eyes and clenched her hands into fists, her nails cutting her skin. She wanted to lose it on Taylor so badly she could taste it. For now, the balled-up covers she was strangling would have to do.

"Just go," she said calmly.

She waited for her bedroom door to close before rolling over and releasing everything she had into her pillow. Her screams somersaulted into cursing sobs, aimed at those stupid, stupid girls, the same ones she'd once thought were so important—starting with evil Gillian, who'd wanted her forever silenced, and ending with Taylor, the selfish bitch who didn't have a clue what she had done, who was too thick and self-absorbed to ever get it.

She rolled onto her back, resting her hands behind her head, feeling spent and tired of it all. She stared at her bedroom ceiling, counting the cracks and thinking she'd like to change the color of her room. *Just a bunch of doofuses.*

She got up and took a shower.

CHAPTER 44

HANNAH PULLED THE PHONE INTO HER ROOM, CLOSING her door. At the sound of his voice, her nervousness almost made her hang up. Instead, she let go of her stuffed hippo and decided to go for it.

"Peter? Hi." Her brain suddenly blanked; she looked to her Christopher Atkins poster on the wall for help. "Ah, so . . . I-I just wanted to thank you . . . for saving my life," she finally managed in a small voice that didn't sound like hers. She cleared her throat. *What am I doing?* She'd been thinking about Peter, wondering how he was after that night. She'd lost track of him after he tackled Toby. They both could have been killed, and she'd been the one to drag him into it. She twisted the phone cord through her fingers, walking in circles around her room.

"So, about everything . . . if you hadn't been there . . . I wouldn't be . . ."

"Hannah, I didn't save you."

"What?"

"I didn't do anything. You saved yourself."

"I don't . . ." She could hear Peter exhaling into the phone and wished she could see his face.

"When Toby turned the gun on you, Deacon was still moving on the ground, but Toby wouldn't let you go to him, remember?" Hannah felt like she was watching a movie as she sat down on the edge of her bed and listened as Peter retold the nightmare. As he did, it all flooded back—including the words she'd used to subdue Toby, distracting him, before *she* pulled the gun from his hands. *She* had been the one to sail it into the lake. Not Peter.

"'Bout the time your father got there, those two guys, who said they were cops, showed up in that white car and took Deacon away. Before the ambulance arrived. It was weird," Peter said.

Hannah nodded, barely remembering their faces. The details from that horrific night she'd unconsciously buried. Now it felt like it had happened to someone else.

They ended up staying on the phone for a while. Peter was so easy to talk to, and it felt good to release some of her guilt from that night. His perspective filled in the holes for her and lessened the nagging anxiety she'd been feeling that she could have done more to prevent Deacon's death. Patiently, he rehashed all the details of that night with her over and over again, and for that she was grateful. With him, she never needed to explain.

Hannah caught her reflection in her movie star mirror and watched herself twirling her hair while on the phone with a boy—her friend. "Want to come over and watch a movie later?" she asked on a whim, surprising herself.

She smiled as she hung up and rose to get dressed.

Hannah spent the following weeks reading in her room from a growing stack of books supplied by Peter. She didn't know why he kept loaning her books, but she was glad for it. She found solace in writing in her diary and listening to music, too—mostly to avoid doing homework, even though she was finding school easy again.

It hadn't taken as long as she'd thought it would for the whispers and stares to die down at school. She had winter break to thank for that. Pretty soon after the semester started, it seemed, the entire student body was off concerning itself with the latest big high school drama.

Sometimes the sadness would creep back into her heart without warning; the radio would play one of their songs, and the jagged pain of him being gone would dive right back into her chest. When she just needed to remember Deacon, to feel him again, she'd pull out from underneath her bed a purple shoebox. She'd written their initials, H and D, on it, and dubbed it her "HAD" box. Inside were mementos of the darkly romantic, undeniably sexy boy she would always love, including the dried white rose he'd given her after their first fight, the only note he'd ever written her—the one warning about Gillian's trap for her in the park—the newspaper article about his death, and the small pink polka-dotted diary with a heart-shaped lock in which she had recorded their brief three months together.

Flipping through the pages, Hannah could decipher her mood immediately by her handwriting, from blissfully happy to crying her eyes out. The later entries were the most erratic, filled with mounting angst and worry, always worry. She seemed constantly at odds with herself, questioning his genuineness and her insecurities about why he was with her. Thankfully, she didn't feel like that girl now.

The more Deacon had dealt, especially when it came to the heavier stuff he'd started bringing back from the city toward the end, the more distant he had become. It hadn't mattered what they felt for one another; the drugs had always come first. Like the day she found them: several plastic sandwich bags brimming with small, jagged rocks, off-white in color, stashed in the back of her bottom dresser drawer. They'd spoken volumes as she flushed them, one by one, down the toilet.

But still at night she dreamed of Deacon. Beyond her overwhelming sense of loss, there was an intense love and gratitude surrounding her memories of him. Deacon was the one who had changed everything. Good and bad, wild and tortured, he had given her real beauty, the beauty she couldn't see in herself. *I like you like this.*

And maybe, just maybe, she'd given him the peace he sought as well. How he'd longed for his parents' attention and love. Just like Hannah. Perhaps in their short time together, she had given him what he'd craved: love and understanding from someone who was as broken and desperate inside as he was—just as tortured by obsessions and compulsions it seemed no one else would understand.

She knew that beneath his outward beauty had lived a trapped, caring boy with a longing, dark heart. Inside the black armor of his don't-mess-with-me clothing and ultracool persona had lived someone wanting to be loved—just like her. He hadn't seen her acne and lame hair. Instead, he'd looked into her eyes and kissed her soul.

"I loved you at your darkest," she whispered.

EPILOGUE

As a kid—prior to his parents' separation, before his world bottomed out—Deacon used to watch in rapt fascination as his father cleaned and hand-polished his prized gun collection. His mother would be off somewhere, her obsessive-compulsive energy temporarily removed from the house for a few hours, granting the two of them a shared solitude that was magical.

His father would softly whistle over the classical music playing low in the room while he lined up each gun case across his massive desk under the glow of the green bankers lamp. Deacon was allowed to open the cases one by one, each with a unique locking mechanism that made him feel important and smart. He'd take a step back after the last one, hold his breath, and watch his father survey his "babies" while he listened to the logs pop in the fireplace.

His father told colorful stories, each one larger than the last, revealing the natural southern drawl that he hid from the public as he spoke. Affectionately, he referred to each rifle or pistol as "her" and "she." Some had been passed down in his family from Civil War days. The small, shiny, modern one was usually left out of the case and tucked in the top drawer of his father's desk. Deacon was never allowed to touch it or be in the study without his father. But he never listened.

At fourteen, when Deacon returned to live with Kingsley,

he'd found the drawer unlocked. He'd rarely touched the small pistol, however; the mystique of it had faded by then, along with everything else from his early childhood days. The Friday of the shooting, he wanted to take it with him on his city run, since he wasn't going to risk the "Barbie and Ken" shield after last time's near disaster with Jade. But he found the drawer empty.

He never made it into the city; instead, he found Jade outside his house that morning, too strung out to stand, and immediately he knew that something was happening; he could feel it. He forced her to talk, and soon she was relaying Gillian's whole plan—babbling about how it involved Toby, and revealing its ultimate target, his one weakness. *Hannah.*

God, how he loved the way she looked that night with her wild hair lit up under the park lights, her face still incredibly loving. *She must care or she wouldn't have shown*, he thought when he saw her. He was so sure that he had it all under control. Toby was a joke. He could take care of everything, and then Hannah wouldn't have to worry. He'd prove himself to her. Prove his love. But he hadn't seen the gun coming. How the hell *did* Toby get their father's gun?

A clean hit, one doctor said.

Lucky, the other one told him.

Do this, and we won't go after the girl, those cops said standing over his hospital bed, somewhere outside of town.

He could see her now when he closed his eyes, feel her presence as he walked up the path to his old dorm under the humming of the street lamps. "Soon," he whispered into the night air. The thought of her was the one thing sustaining him. *She's still in love; I can feel it.*

The door opened before he had a chance to knock. "D . . . good to see you, been a long time, man."

"Thomas."

acknowledgments

Thank you to my early readers, diehard believers, and fearless cheerleaders, especially Caitlin McCarthy, Lauren Longwell, Linda Lowe, Kristen McManus, Shelbi Brennan, and Isla Brennan.

For Isabelle Herbrich, Robin Coyle, Laura Emmert, Patty Skahill, Sarah Stites, and Beth Foster, who knew me when and still love me today.

For Mom, Dad, Tommy, Andy, and Danny, who raised me well. And to the Cumiskey-Pulaski-AlFerranto clan, who welcomed me into their loving fold and gave me wings.

I'm blessed beyond words for my dearest New York, Colorado, and North Carolina friends and family who love me just the way I am and encouraged me to finally do this! You all know who you are, but text me if you don't.

For my Wit, Wine & Wisdom sisters, who make me braver every day.

To my generous teacher and mentor at Gotham Writers, Julie Chibbaro, who ignited the match that became *I Like You Like This*. And to those who made the fire burn brighter, especially the gifted Jaime Karnes and my fellow Gotham classmates.

To my amazing publisher, Brooke Warner, project manager, Cait Levin, and all my She Writes Press sisters, especially Dorit Sasson, Susan Hadler, Nicole Waggoner, and Anna Gatmon, who guided me along the way.

For my fearless editors, Krissa Lagos and Megan Rynott,

whose kind insight helped craft the story of Hannah and Deacon into a better one.

A big shout-out to my wondrous publicity team at Book-Sparks, especially Crystal Patriarche and Morgan Rath. To Maggie Ruf at SparkPoint Studio for a beautiful website. And to Kristin Bustamante at BookSparks for her fabulous graphics.

Thank you to Julie Metz at She Writes Press for the lovely cover, and to my niece, Beth Pulaski, for the wonderful profile picture.

I'm grateful for the unwavering support from my favorite guys: Mac, Finn, and Fletcher.

Finally, for Mark, my biggest supporter and hero and the one who holds my hand through everything. In the crook of your arm is where I belong. Always.

about the author

Heather Cumiskey is a freelance writer and editor. She studied English at State University of New York at Albany. *I Like You Like This* is her debut novel. She resides in Maryland with her husband and three sons.

SELECTED TITLES FROM SHE WRITES PRESS

She Writes Press is an independent publishing
company founded to serve women writers everywhere.
Visit us at www.shewritespress.com.

How to Grow an Addict by J.A. Wright. $16.95, 978-1-63152-991-7. Raised by an abusive father, a detached mother, and a loving aunt and uncle, Randall Grange is built for addiction. By twenty-three, she knows that together, pills and booze have the power to cure just about any problem she could possibly have . . . right.

Beautiful Garbage by Jill DiDonato. $16.95, 978-1-938314-01-8. Talented but troubled young artist Jodi Plum leaves suburbia for the excitement of the city—and is soon swept up in the sexual politics and downtown art scene of 1980s New York.

Cleans Up Nicely by Linda Dahl. $16.95, 978-1-938314-38-4. The story of one gifted young woman's path from self-destruction to self-knowledge, set in mid-1970s Manhattan.

Keep Her by Leora Krygier. $16.95, 978-1-63152-143-0. When a water main bursts in rain-starved Los Angeles, seventeen-year-old artist Maddie and filmmaker Aiden's worlds collide in a whirlpool of love and loss. Is it meant to be?

The Rooms Are Filled by Jessica Null Vealitzek. $16.95, 978-1-938314-58-2. The coming-of-age story of two outcasts—a nine-year-old boy who just lost his father, and a closeted young woman—brought together by circumstance.

An Address in Amsterdam by Mary Dingee Fillmore. $16.95, 978-1-63152-133-1. After facing relentless danger and escalating raids for 18 months, Rachel Klein—a well-behaved young Jewish woman who transformed herself into a courier for the underground when the Nazis invaded her country—persuades her parents to hide with her in a dank basement, where much is revealed.

CPSIA information can be obtained
at www.ICGtesting.com
Printed in the USA
BVOW08s1940020218
506946BV00003B/10/P

9 781631 522925